# Quick as a Wink

Also by Virgilio Goncalves and published by Ginninderra Press
*Stings in Tails*

Virgilio Goncalves

# Quick as a Wink

# Acknowledgements

Thanks to Lesley, for her patience.

Also to Alan Clark, for his editing suggestions, and Andrew Morgan
for the thorough read-through.

To the University of the Third Age (Aldinga) creative writers –
without you, these sixty stories might not have been written.

*Quick as a Wink*
ISBN 978 1 76041 935 6
Copyright © Virgilio Goncalves 2020
Cover photo: Julissa Helmuth from Pexels

First published 2020 by
**GINNINDERRA PRESS**
PO Box 3461 Port Adelaide 5015
www.ginninderrapress.com.au

# Contents

# Foreword

You've got ten minutes to spare before your appointment.

Should you unpack the dishwasher?
Iron those jeans?
Make the bed?
Clean the dog's bowl?

No.

Pour yourself a cuppa, and snatch
*Quick as a Wink*
off your coffee table.

Immerse yourself in a

recess

to

recollect,

recoil,

reminisce

or smile.

You'll be pleased you chose not to do those chores.
But you might be late for that appointment.

# Never Alone

'My daddy always plays that song,' Telene told her best friend, Felicia, as she poured the pretend tea into her friend's cup.

Telene was a big girl now – almost eight – but she was always happy to play with her best friend. Felicia wasn't really a best friend. Felicia was her imaginary friend, the one Telene loved more than anybody in the whole wide world.

Except for her daddy, of course.

'You know why he always plays that song?' Telene asked Felicia. 'Well, I'll tell you why, Felicia, just like I've told you all those times before. You have a really bad memory, Felicia. You're very lucky I have a lot of patience.'

She smiled, exposing a crooked front tooth. 'I learnt that word from Daddy the other day, when he was speaking about Mummy.'

Telene, dressed in a light blue dress, and pastel pink shoes and socks, got up from around the yellow table in the cubby house her father had built. She wanted to adjust the chair on which Felicia was sitting. Of course, no one was sitting there.

'There you are, Felicia. That's better. You're sitting upright, just the way Daddy says children should always sit,' said Telene, pulling her own shoulders back as she sat in her chair.

'I was talking about that song Daddy always plays, the one with the words "Where do you go to my lovely?"'

Telene undid the elastic band that tied up her straight, black hair – then tightened it again so the hair pulled back neatly from her white-as-a-cloud complexion.

'My daddy,' Telene said to Felicia, 'loves that song because, like I said, it reminds him of Mummy. He told me Mummy always used to like diamonds and pearls in her hair and always wanted to marry a millionaire. You know what that is, Felicia? A millionaire? It's someone who has lots of money. Not like us.'

Telene rubbed a blob of lipstick into her left cheek. She'd found the lipstick in her father's drawer a few months before. He'd never had the heart to throw it away even though it had been three years since his wife walked out of their modest home one afternoon – and never returned.

'Daddy said that Mummy wanted a racehorse for Christmas which she would keep just for a laugh,' Telene told Felicia, 'and she also wanted to live in a fancy apartment where she could keep her Rolling Stones records, whatever they are.'

Telene's father was sure his wife had walked out on her family because he could not give her what she'd wanted. From a humble home, he'd been forced to leave school when he was young and managed to bring home some money from a job he'd had washing dishes in a one-star hotel.

He was surprised she'd married him. He had no prospects but he was strong, handsome and kind – and she'd been desperate to leave her home because of the abuse she'd suffered from her stepfather.

Just like in the song, Telene's mother dreamed of sipping Napoleon brandy, talking like Marlene Dietrich and dancing like Zizi Jeanmaire. After realising Telene's father would never give her that life, she'd simply walked away, leaving him and Telene to fend for themselves. She'd never left a note.

'Daddy still loves Mummy,' Telene told Felicia. 'She's his princess. He says she always will be. Daddy doesn't think Mummy will come back, because she's a dreamer. She dreams of things that will never happen to her.'

Telene paused to take a sip of her imaginary tea, not forgetting to stick out two small fingers so she could hold the cup like a lady. Her father had shown her how to do it. Telene was as proud as a mother hen the day she got it right.

'I think Mummy may come back one day,' she said to Felicia. 'When she finds out what a beautiful girl I have become, Mummy may come back. I'll let you see her too, Felicia, when she does come back.'

A knock on the cubby house door startled the little girl.

'You there, honey?' Telene's father asked.

'Yes, Daddy. Do you want to come in and have tea with Felicia and me?'

'It's getting on, honey. I've made a sandwich for you at the big house. It's in the kitchen.'

'Can Felicia come too, Daddy?'

'Of course she can.' Telene's father waited for his daughter to climb out of the cubby.

'I'll hold this hand so you can hold Felicia by the other hand, just in case she trips and falls,' Telene said.

When they reached the kitchen, Telene asked, 'Did you make Felicia a sandwich too, Daddy?'

'Of course I did, honey, with her usual Vegemite.'

'I'm so lucky you're my daddy,' Telene told her father.

'I'm so lucky to have you too, my darling,' he replied, clutching his daughter close to his chest, the way a child hugs a doll.

'I'll never be alone, Daddy,' Telene said, 'because I know I'll always have you and Felicia with me…and, even though she's not here now, I know my lovely mummy will be with me too, one day…'

# Letting Go

Celeste Rayner was exhilarated and agitated – at the same time. It had been a long nine months, but the time had come. Eventually. Celeste thought about the battle she'd fought to get to this moment. It had been hard work, but she knew it would be worth every minute of the time she'd spent in the lead-up to this momentous occasion. She'd planned it all, mostly on her own. She was proud of herself for doing that. Now that it was about to happen, she felt she deserved to be rewarded for her meticulous preparation. And the celebration would be as joyful as the christening of any new arrival.

*

From the beginning, Celeste knew it was best to keep exercising throughout the nine months. She'd been advised it would keep her on track, so she maintained a regimen that would have pleased any fitness coach. There were zumba and yoga classes, meditation and massage sessions, long walks, bicycle rides, swimming in the sea or in a pool. Every afternoon, she'd spent doing some form of exercise. Celeste was convinced she didn't need a personal trainer to tell her what was right or wrong. She knew, instinctively.

It was the same with her food. Celeste ate with as much zest as any maturing mother but it was all healthy: vegies, a little meat – always without any of the bad fat – and fruit. Probably her favourite food during this time was bananas. If she flagged at any stage, she peeled from a bunch she always had on hand. They kept her energy levels up. She needed them high to achieve optimal results.

She did have the occasional wine with her evening meals, but it never became a habit. She'd given up smoking early into the journey. She knew if she didn't give it up, she'd chain-smoke her way through the nine months. That would not lead to the best outcome.

Celeste also was fortunate she slept well. It was rare for people in such situations to have a good night's rest, but she'd always been a sound sleeper. On the odd occasion, she awoke in the middle of the night. She made sure, however, that a notebook rested on her bedside table to enable her to jot down whatever was keeping her awake. The pressing problem would be there, in scrawled script, for her to deal with in the morning.

Celeste was forthright with her mentor, Margaret Watson, about her hours of work. She'd told Margaret it was five hours a day, every day, nine a.m. until two p.m., including weekends. Not a minute more. Once she'd done her five hours, she'd switch off her computer. Celeste was determined to work right up until B-Day, as she liked to call the due date. If necessary, she'd told Margaret, she'd be ready to tackle extra days if unforeseen problems led to any delay.

'I'll do what it takes,' she told Margaret. 'I don't want to have any regrets.'

Celeste, however, was already dealing with one regret. She would not have a partner with whom to share her big moment. She'd decided a long time ago ex-boyfriend Steve Joyce would not be the man to support her when she'd most need it.

'I love him,' she'd told her worried mum. 'But he can't handle things when there's a little hiccup. If he can't handle the pressure now, there's little chance he'll do it when the time comes, when all the attention will be on me. So what's the point?'

As with any expectant woman, Celeste anguished over this for a time. It was a big step to take by yourself when you had your whole life ahead of you, but she could handle it. She was motivated, determined and energetic. It would be easy, she convinced herself.

*

The day of the momentous occasion emerged. Celeste, exhilarated and agitated, had woken up sweating. Profusely. Hours later, as she drove herself up to the centre for the arrival, she was still perspiring. She couldn't fathom it. She'd done the hard yards. There was nothing to fear. She tried to convince herself she'd done all the right things. The preparation was perfect.

Why the angst?

As she entered the room, behind which she knew her family and friends would congregate to congratulate her, Celeste's first thoughts were that it looked bare, sterile.

Her eyes moved to a large box. It lay sealed on what to her looked like an operating table. She turned to Margaret, her mentor and also her new best friend, then ran at her, imploring, 'No, don't open the box…I can't do this.'

'Celeste, don't be silly,' Margaret said, quietly but firmly. 'You've laboured on this for such a long time, for nine months solid. It's time to let go…'

Quickly, with the help of a knife as sharp as a scalpel, Celeste slashed at the tape that secured the cardboard box, then yelled in delight as the lid fell open. 'At last, at last – the birth of my first novel!'

# Nature's Call

All was quiet in the veldt. It was the silence before the kill.

Only the group knew it, though. The five members knew it because, to them, this was nothing new. They were old hands at what lay ahead. However, their intended victim was unaware of the peril. This was to be his first taste of danger. It might also be his last.

Night had spread rapidly, like an ink spill on pale paper. Clouds concealed both moon and stars, making the evening as black as death. It also made it even more difficult for the giraffe to see.

For the female lions, however, nocturnal hunting was best. They had picked up the scent when their prey, six times the height of any lioness, had split from the tower of giraffes, languid and lazy, which had chomped at leaves, chock-full of juice, from the acacia trees in the African bush.

It wasn't long before the pride had herded the lone giraffe out of the trees into a clearing. There were no prompts, but they worked as a team. Had they been human, you might have imagined them in earlier conference, discussing options.

'We'll use the siege strategy,' one could have said.

'Once we've got him in the open, we'll encircle him,' another might have added.

'Then, while the rest of us distract him, one will attack,' a third would have concluded.

The queens of the animal world, however, did not have to confer. They prided themselves on know-how, discipline and an instinct so sharp that each knew what she would have to do when the time came.

Most of the pride were jungle-wise. All knew the giraffe's legs were his weapons. He could kick with vigour, using fore and hind legs. They knew, from previous experience, or perhaps from a chinwag around their places of rest, that those long legs could maim. Even kill. So they were wary.

But the pride was confident, too. They knew they had weapons of their own. They could rely on their powerful forelimbs and retractable claws that could clutch onto their prey for long periods, claws which left sets of parallel incisions on their victims, like fingernails dragged through thick-set mud.

During one of their gatherings, the lionesses must have worked together, too, to remind each other they should only attack from behind. The skin on the necks and front of giraffes was almost as thick as an abandoned tree trunk – much more difficult to penetrate than its butt.

'Biting off the tail would be a good start,' another of the pride might have said, without a shred of malice. For them, it was Nature doing what Nature did best. Survival of the fittest. And, for the pride, they were usually the fittest – and smartest.

*

It was time. Amid snarls, the now-encircled giraffe kicked out aimlessly as the lionesses moved in and out, around his hooves. In a flash, one of the pride, finding herself in the perfect spot, launched at the giraffe's rear, got a good grip with her sharp teeth and used her claws to injure her victim. The scenario repeated itself as a lioness became fatigued and a replacement got a grip.

The pride, however, was becoming weary. Perhaps, they might have thought, tonight would not be their night. Perhaps the giraffe, though hurt, might get another chance.

There was an uneasy truce. Still, the big cats circled their limping prey.

Suddenly, louder roars filled the killing field. A coalition of young male lions had unexpectedly entered the arena. Fresh and eager, with slabs of extra muscle, they attacked ferociously, finishing off what their older, female counterparts had begun. It was as if the coalition knew there was a meal to be had – and it was their time to pay their respects and reward the mature lionesses who had nurtured them when they were cubs.

*

All was quiet again in the bush. It was the silence after the kill – and the feed.

The group, bloated and content, had always known it would end this way. They knew not only because they were arrogant. They knew because, as with other prides and coalitions before them, they'd worked as a team of well-disciplined and instinctive creatures to prove yet again which beast was chief of the jungle.

For the casualty, that first sample of danger was his last. But he would not be the final victim in the veldt, where Nature decides who gets to have their meal on any given day – and who gets to be the meal.

# Face of Forgiveness

She stood erect, serene and proud against the backdrop of lush green hills. She looked over the never-ending ocean. It was certainly content to have her cast an eye over its ceaselessly cascading waves. Though not of body nor flesh, she seemed lifelike enough, two well-proportioned fingers of her right hand resting delicately on a well-defined thumb while the remaining two fingers appeared to be addressing all around her with a peace salute.

At any time, I expected the Goddess of Mercy, newly cemented on Sellicks Hill, to give me a wink…

*

I was alone. I'd snuck over the boundary fence to her enclosure late that afternoon. No one else was in sight.

I wandered over to where she proudly stood. I squeezed through another barrier around her. I'd brought my climbing gear, intent on achieving my goal: I wanted to see exactly what she was peering at – from her exact spot.

I clambered up where her podgy legs would have been had they not been covered (to preserve her modesty) by a glamorous, ornate gown. I clasped my arms around where knobbly knees might have protruded, then gently threw another rope around her neck. There was no intention to harm her.

The granite started to cool in the winter sun. I lifted myself to where her tummy might have been. Just above that lay her other hand, clutching something. Was it an urn?

I turned and looked out at a sight so spectacular it was little wonder my new lady friend's lips resembled a smile of satisfaction, deep and lasting.

As the sun peeped out for one last look before bedding down for the night, the day's exertions got the better of me. Comfortably ensconced within her breast, like a babe in arms, I must have dozed off.

*

'Here, mate, here.'

I heard the voice. It was bossy, but squeaked, as if still attempting that extra step into adulthood.

'Comin', mate, comin',' was the response, indisputably ocker.

I looked down. It was long past dusk. I could barely make out the outlines of the figures at the base of the eighteen-metre-tall granite statue. They had not spotted me because night had quickly spread its dark-ink tentacles around its captured audience.

'Got the cans?' I heard Squeaky ask.

'Yep – all three of them buggers,' replied Ocker.

'Let's get going, mate,' Squeaky urged. 'We've got a way to climb, then we can have some fun, turning this piece of bull crap into a masterpiece of cool art.'

'Want me to flick the torch yet?' Ocker asked.

'Better not,' said Squeaky. 'Might still be some nosies prancing around. Don't want to bust our cover.'

My heart skipped numerous beats. I knew what they were up to. And the outcome wouldn't be pretty. The Goddess (aka the Buddha monument at Sellicks) was in for a facelift she didn't need.

Right now, though, I was more concerned about what would happen when the invaders and I came face to face. This seemed inevitable. There was no place for me to go…and Squeaky and Ocker were moving up. It was a question of what I would do to defuse the commotion when they reached their destination.

'OK, buddy, the torch, shine the torch,' demanded Squeaky.

'No worries,' replied Ocker.

As he did so, my screeching 'Aiiiiyyyyeee' shattered the stillness. Though it came from the heavens, it was more like a cry from the devil.

Within seconds, Squeaky and Ocker were on their butts, out of the Goddess's fenced perimeter and, at a guess, scrambling like two startled bucks out of the building enclosure. Not more than a minute later, I heard a ute rev, then roar away into the night.

I grinned, relieved. I grasped the car key in the top pocket of my shirt and flicked on the tiny torchlight attached to the key. It shone over the urn held in my lady's left hand. A scrap of paper, unnoticed before, hung limply at its opening. I grabbed it, unfolded it, and read the words scrawled on it: 'Forgive your young brothers for they know not what they do.'

I shone the light further up to the face of the Goddess of Mercy. It might have been the mix of lighting and shadow playing tricks, but her smile seemed to have broadened – and, this time, she surely winked.

# How the Mighty Fell

Blake Rawbone was a big, brawny man. He was also used to getting his own way. That wasn't because he was smart, talented or skilled. It was because he'd been fortunate to have been born into money. His grandfather had made millions in the property market. When he'd died, Blake's father took over the vast portfolio. Three years later, Blake's dad had died of a heart attack, leaving his only son as the heir.

Blake was well known in Providence, the South Australian town in which he lived. Face to face, locals deferred to him. However, behind his back, he was referred to as Blake the Bully.

He lived alone because no woman would put up with his contempt for other people, particularly those not as well-off as he. Blake was the self-appointed boss of the town and had more clout than any mayor.

Because his coffers overflowed with riches made by others, Blake travelled widely, particularly to the US. Las Vegas was his favourite place. When he arrived back in Providence after another trip there, he brought with him one more cowboy hat; another solid gold chain to hang around his gaudy, open-to-the-navel shirts; one more glittering ring to add to his collection, many on all fingers of both hands; and his signature cigars, which he smoked where he liked, regardless of non-smoking signs in most eating places. No one was game enough to turf him out of these locations as Blake either owned the building, the restaurant, or he was the licensee.

It was ironic that Blake's fall from grace would occur in one of these buildings.

*

It happened in the quaint French restaurant tucked away obscurely on the fourth floor of one of the tallest buildings in the otherwise small town. The eating house was popular with locals and sought after by tourists. This was mainly because of its mild-mannered, skinny little chef, Arnoldo Pezzance, who also managed the restaurant, serving meals strictly at lunchtimes only.

Blake Rawbone had not eaten at all the day he ignored the 'Closed' sign on the door of the French restaurant, well past lunchtime. He had had a big night of card playing, and umpteen glasses of rum and coke, with local property developers he'd impelled to play on into the early hours of that morning.

'Arnoldo! Get me a steak!' Blake boomed, his massive frame squeezing through the double doors of the restaurant.

Arnoldo, who had been quietly rereading his favourite novel after the rush of lunchtime, was vexed by this intrusion. Cursing mildly under his breath, he placed the book in the large, front pocket of his apron. 'Monsieur Blake, I don't think this is possible…' he stammered.

'Now! I'm up for a thick, juicy one, medium-rare as usual, with hot mustard – don't worry about veg,' Blake roared, drawing a chair and plonking his Vegas-styled boots on a table which Arnoldo had recently set.

The Frenchman did not like confrontation. However, he had always been astute. He decided to fry up a steak to get the bully off his premises, quickly. Without his usual care, he rustled up a thick fillet with the required condiment and placed it in front of his unwanted customer.

Within seconds, Blake the Bully roared. 'What the hell is this, Arnoldo?'

'The steak you asked for, monsieur.'

'This isn't cooked!'

'It's what you asked for, monsieur.'

'No, it's bloody well not. Fix it!'

Arnoldo stooped in the face of this abuse. Then, as if spurred on by countless intimidated chefs around the world, he straightened up. Quietly, he said, 'You take it like it is – or you can leave my restaurant.'

Seconds of silence were filled with fright.

'Fix it! I said fix it!' screamed Blake the Bully.

'No!'

'What?' Blake swiftly lifted his feet off the table and, as quickly, stretched his ample frame so it towered above the little chef. 'What did you just say?'

Arnoldo realised he might have taken his resolve a little too far. He turned quickly, then darted up three flights of stairs to the safety of the balcony. He did not anticipate that the bully would follow. In the brief scuffle which ensued, Arnoldo found himself hanging by his fingertips from the edge of the balcony.

*

At that moment I looked up, horrified to see a man hanging precariously from the hotel balcony. I identified Arnoldo immediately. I also recognised Blake. In a fury, the bully was attempting, with the heels of his boots, to smash the fingers of the dangling chef. Then, with the dexterity of a trapeze artiste, I watched Arnoldo grab Blake's ankle with one hand. The bigger man stumbled, cartwheeled, then plummeted four floors to the concrete below.

I rushed to where he had fallen. Next to the body of the prone Blake lay a book. It was the one Arnoldo had been reading, the one tucked away in his apron, the book he loved to read and read again, the novel entitled *The Power of One*.

# Second Best

Chantal was in despair. She'd been dumped again. And the timing was terrible.

It was just five days before her brother's wedding, at which she was to be one of the bridesmaids. She did not want to turn up to the reception clinging to the arm of one of her brother's friends. She'd always said she'd take someone she knew and liked, not someone loaned to her for a day by her brother. She liked her brother, but his mates were as desirable as the last drunken bums left standing in a squalid pub.

Why? Chantal asked herself. Why does this always happen to me? Chantal knew the answer. She knew she had a problem but, she reminded herself, she would never, ever admit it to anyone.

On the face of it, Chantal shouldn't have been in this predicament. She had the looks of a Charlie's Angel, the figure of a swimsuit model, and enough nous to become a teacher. She also had an easy-going disposition, on the outside at least. The perfect all-rounder, everyone said.

But Chantal also had that hidden past, the problem she hoped would go away, but never did. It crept up on her, resurfaced as unsuspectingly as an unwanted pregnancy.

*

'So, who're you bringing to the wedding?' her brother, Jackson, asked.

'Not sure, now that Simon's no longer on the scene,' said Chantal.

'Why not Matt down the street?' said Jackson.

'Hmmm, maybe – a bit short for me,' said Chantal.

'It's just for a day.'

'Yeah, but we'd look funny together.'

'Reminder, sister dear: I'm the star attraction on Saturday. Not you.'

'Yeah, but…'

'But nothing…'

'You're right. I'll head down there now.'

Though she knew Matt, Chantal was anxious. She never liked that feeling. It was when the problem arose. She did not want to revisit that dilemma.

She strode, with the conviction of a successful sales rep, down the street. 'Anyone home?' she asked, her persistent door-knocking bringing no reply. 'Hello? Anyone there?' she repeated.

There was a reason Matt hadn't replied, she frowned as she walked back to her brother's house. He doesn't want to be seen with me, she told herself. He couldn't be bothered with someone like me.

'Stop it!' she scolded herself loudly. 'Don't do this to yourself.'

*

'Any luck?' asked her brother later that day.

'No. And I've decided to give him a miss,' said Chantal. 'Think I'll ask Andy Rennert instead.'

'The butcher's son? You're kidding, Chantal. That's scraping the barrel.'

'He's tall, a looker and he's got big biceps – just my kind of guy.'

'He's also a psycho. He carries a knife wherever he goes.'

'Rubbish – that's just gossip. Have you ever seen him with it?'

'Can't say I have, but one of my mates did.'

Chantal sighed. This was becoming a strain. Her insecurities flooded back. She didn't want that. She knew what would happen if she let them in – if she allowed them in, she'd start again. She didn't want that. It wouldn't do her any good.

'This is a simple situation,' she told her brother. 'I have a wedding to go to. I want to take someone I like. And seeing you think the butcher's son is unsuitable, I'll ask someone else.'

'And who will that be?' asked her brother, finally bored by his sister's indecision.

'Simon, at the pub,' said Chantal.

Jackson roared his irritating laugh. 'Good luck with that,' he told Chantal. 'You and how many others will be chasing him for a date? You'll probably be sixth in line.'

Chantal fled the room. She was in her car before her brother had a chance to assess his thoughtless response.

Soon, Chantal was at her apartment, her haven. She shut, then deadlocked the front door. She switched off her mobile phone. She tried to calm down. But she was way past rational thinking.

'I'm useless,' she shouted. 'Always have been, always will be. Mum was right. I should've been born a boy. She always wanted another boy. Not me. She told me she didn't want me. She said she asked the adoption people for a boy. Instead, she got me.'

There was no letting up. Chantal was in rant mode. 'Mum took me in because she felt sorry for me. She always regretted it. And she was right. I'm useless. I was useless on the farm and I'm still useless. I'm nothing. Nothing.'

Chantal walked purposefully toward her room. It had been a long time coming. But she knew what she needed to do. It was as clear as a lightning strike at night. It was time to rid herself of the angst, the stress, the pain. There was only one way to do that. And she knew how to do it.

Sitting on her bed, she unlocked, then slid open the door of her bedside cabinet. She placed a hand inside the space – and, gently, with the fondness of a parent embracing a long-lost child, Chantal pulled out one of the three bottles of brandy.

# Love at First Flight

I knew it was a gamble. But we had no option. This was our chance to escape. Even if Charlotte, or I, was left behind.

*

That scenario emerged sometime after I'd decided I'd had enough. I'd been homesick. I'd moved to Adelaide with my carers, as I call them. I wasn't happy about going to the city. I wanted to stay in the country. In Whyalla. It was my home. I'd lived there since I'd been born. But the carers thought they knew better. They still do. It's frustrating. They're frustrating. I know they care, though. In their own way.

Anyway, I'd been missing Whyalla. And my mates there. I decided the only way to get back was to leave. Just take off. I didn't need luggage. I sort of knew the way. If I got lost, someone would find me or give me a lift. And take me there.

So, one morning, I did it. I walked out the front door. Didn't even look back. Mind you, I had a good feed before I left. Just in case.

It wasn't long before an old guy in his sedan felt sorry for me and picked me up. I'd been struggling, I admit. Whyalla was a little further than I thought.

The kids in the car were all over me like a horrible rash.

'He's adorable, Daddy,' said the girl.

'Can we keep him?' asked the boy.

'We'll drop him off with someone when we get to Pirie,' said the old guy.

Port Pirie, did he say? Good, that's on the way, I thought.

Geez, the kids couldn't stop touching me. I was irritated. I'm a dog.

I don't mind cuddling and hugging, but they were holding me as tightly as a little girl clutches her favourite doll. I was hot and bothered from the walk, and these two knee-high tearaways were suffocating me.

So I jumped. 'Course I waited till the car had slowed at one of the small towns you go through. When it did, I jumped out of the window and ran into the bush. I was free – and they weren't going to get me back.

I slept overnight near a waterhole, after rummaging for some local fare and hoping it wouldn't make me sick. I was by the roadside early next morning.

It wasn't long before my next lift. I wasn't sure about this guy. But, before I knew it, I'd been bundled into the back of his panel van. With all the other mongrels. There would've been a dozen of them. All mongrels. Except for one.

Charlotte.

Cute as candyfloss. And as fluffy. She scrubbed up like a catwalk queen. Long eyelashes and big, brown eyes. There was instant attraction.

I read fear in those eyes too, however. It seemed she'd been dognapped. By the driver of the panel van. Which meant I was a victim, too.

Our destination? Not Whyalla. Asia. Either as a dog delicacy or dog fighter. That was the natter from the mongrels.

I couldn't imagine either option for Charlotte. So we found a quiet spot away from the mixed breed. And we hatched a plan.

It was pretty simple. When the van next stopped, as soon as the rear door opened, we'd make our getaway. Easy as that.

When we put it into action, it worked to perfection…except for one major detail.

The van came to a standstill. The rear door opened slightly. We jumped. Together.

Charlotte and me.

Me and Charlotte.

But…only one of us got away.

It wasn't Charlotte.

In a flash, before I had time to yelp, the driver had slammed shut the rear door and was gone in a blur of red dust. I worked my little legs as fast as a spinning yo-yo, chasing the van for as long I could.

I didn't have the revs to keep up.

*

I never saw Charlotte again.

For one brief moment, it had been there. Love at first glance. The next, it was gone. She was gone.

Eventually, I made it to Whyalla. Saw my mates. Yarned a lot. Played up a bit. Spent a couple of weeks there.

All the while, though I never mentioned it, my heart was breaking.

For Charlotte.

I also decided that my carers would be frantic. They're like that. Caring. Too much so. Anyway, I hit the road again, got back safely, and the carers were as happy to see me as I expected.

Lots of hugs and cuddles.

Gentle ones.

Just like I wanted to give Charlotte.

And get back from her.

# Mum's the Word

It was our energetic mother's eightieth birthday and, for once, the family agreed it was an occasion worth celebrating.

Mum had led a life the iconic actress, Elizabeth Taylor, might have envied. She'd outlived four husbands, guzzled countless gin and tonics as her preferred sundowners in summer, a stout or three in winter, and had smoked a few packets of Marlboro every week since she was sixteen. She'd also had five children, and already had outlasted two of them.

Eleven grandchildren, now adults, completed a life of fertility for the woman known as Big Ethel. She'd got the name, partly because she was one point eight metres tall. Not one of her spouses came anywhere near that. Jack, her last husband, had been the tallest of the lot – at just one point six.

Her size wasn't the only reason Mum was nicknamed Big Ethel. Carrot-coloured hair, a watermelon-sized grin and never without her strawberry lipstick, she also had a personality larger than Queensland's Big Pineapple. After nearly eight decades, she devoured the limelight in any circle of companions.

Mum was known for two other things: she was mischievous and she had a mean streak. Her children thought so anyway.

So when she said she wanted to celebrate her birthday at the Top of the World Restaurant at Mt Lofty and that she was paying, we wondered if she was dinkum. After all, prices for main courses there were bigger than Big Ethel herself. She'd said she wanted us all to enjoy a three-course banquet, plus any drinks we fancied.

We were all invited to the family-only gathering. No excuses were accepted. That meant a table for three of her children, their partners, the eleven grandchildren, six of whom had partners, and, of course, the lady of the moment and her latest man, nicknamed Pee Wee, for reasons that were evident.

A three-course meal for twenty-five people was going to cost more than I thought Big Ethel had in the bank.

'I'm not a pauper, you know,' she said, when I'd asked if she could afford it.

'OK, Mum, it's your shout and you know what you're doing,' I said.

'Yep, and don't you forget it.'

While Mum adored her grandchildren, she didn't think much of her own children, including me. She thought us selfish, self-centred and greedy. I thought my sisters were all of those things, but didn't think I warranted those slurs.

She made it obvious how she felt about her nearest and dearest during a recent conversation. 'You're all hoping I'm gonna kick the bucket soon, aren't you?'

'No, Mum, I hope you live for many more years,' I replied.

'Yeah, yeah. But I've got news for you. I've already written to the Queen telling her to prepare my congratulatory letter for my hundredth birthday.'

'You *will* probably outlive us all,' I said.

'That means you won't see any of my money.'

'Don't expect to, Mum.'

'Ha, you say that – but I know how you and your sisters really feel.'

We'd left it at that and, finally, her special day arrived.

I managed to persuade my sisters – they are a stingy pair! – to share a cab fare for Mum so that she could be taken in style to the venue.

Most of the night was fantastic. The food was high quality and the many bottles of alcohol top notch. The restaurant went to the trouble of providing a cake – no charge! – and staff joined our family to sing 'Happy Birthday' to Mum.

It had been an occasion to remember.

'Bill please,' shouted Mum confidently, as we gathered our belongings to leave.

'Certainly, madam,' said the waitress.

When it arrived, Mum took a cursory glance at the total, which I happened to observe. It read $3,275.

My collar tightened. Sweat lined my forehead. Fingers moistened. I'd had a few, but I was suddenly as sober as the priests who'd married my mother and her sweethearts.

Nonchalantly, Mum plonked her credit card on the plate. As we took turns to plant farewell kisses on her rouged cheeks and to thank her for a wonderful evening, the same waitress rushed back, as breathless as a shopkeeper who'd just wrestled a thief. 'I'm sorry, madam, we cannot accept your credit card,' she mumbled.

Our flame-haired Mum momentarily looked at the waitress with sympathy. Then, through those strawberry-lined lips and in her biggest Big Ethel voice, she broadcast to the room, 'Oh, damn – I must have overdrawn on that account.'

Smiling, she addressed the waitress. 'Not to worry, dear, my generous kids will sort it out.'

# The Killer Dress

Antoinette Bourgeon was the life of any party. She always made an imposing entrance, dressed in red more often than not, with the reddest of lipsticks smothering a wide mouth. She breezed into people's homes. Everyone knew she'd arrived. Her laugh did it. It came from deep in her belly and brought soul into a room the same way hot air invades a floppy balloon and transforms its appearance. She always drew a crowd. She made friends easily and devoured people with her attentiveness. If there was one negative, it was her trusting nature. She saw no wrong in anyone, no matter their nature, looks or dress.

Friends told her she was naïve, that she was easily taken in. They playfully called it her fatal distraction.

'See you at the party tomorrow night,' Antoinette shouted above the din as she left the pub, waving scarlet fingernails at the friends she expected to see again the next night. 'Can't wait to try on the cherry-red kaftan I got in Bali! It's a killer!' she yelled, laughing her laugh.

*

Jason Stockerelli also attracted people. But he didn't appeal to the good people. Instead, scums of society were drawn to him. Jason was also the centre of attention at joints he frequented. His glut of cocaine made him popular. He always had a stash. Characters – mostly muscled, tattooed and previously well-off – spent life savings acquiring the good stuff from Jason.

He didn't stand out in a crowd, but he made up for his short stature with a toned body. He also had a charming smile, which immediately enticed people. With his shaved head, Jason looked like the leader of the pack. He liked that. He liked being in charge, the one calling the shots.

'Catch you boys tomorrow,' Jason told a group of new-found mates, high on booze and cocaine, as he left the pub. He was expecting a big night tomorrow – and even the thought of making a hefty packet right away did not tempt him to linger.

*

'Bugger! Bugger!' Antoinette Bourgeon, in cherry-red kaftan and a matching garland of roses on her head, yelled as her bright red sedan chugged, then stopped as she headed to the party just out of town.

Kicking a tyre in exasperation, Antoinette headed for the closest pub for help. For once, she was on time, so there was no need to phone a friend to tell her she might be late.

'G'day, honey. You're looking uptight…' said the confident voice as Antoinette entered the pub. 'Something bugging you?'

'My car…it's just, just, well…it's given up the ghost.'

'I'm at your service if you need a hand,' the bald, smiling man replied.

'Can you? You sure you don't mind?'

'Sure I'm sure, honey.'

Relieved that help had been near at hand, Antoinette led the man toward her car.

Dusk had fallen. A chill as cold as an ice cube crammed the air.

Antoinette wrapped the warmth of the crimson fabric around her lean body.

Bit of okay, Jason Stockerelli thought as he followed Antoinette to her car. He'd already swigged a six-pack. He was nicely oiled, as he liked to say. He reckoned he was in for a bigger night than he'd thought.

'Let's 'ave a look then, honey. Keys?'

If there was something Jason knew more about than drug dealing, it was cars. And he wasn't afraid to brag about it. 'I'll 'ave it fixed in no time.'

Antoinette was delighted. 'I struck it lucky when I bumped into you,' she said.

*

Within an hour, Antoinette headed toward the party in her repaired vehicle. She was not alone. She was also a passenger. Having convinced her he was free for the night, Jason had elected to drive Antoinette's car.

'Now I can have a big night,' she said.

'As big as you like,' he replied. 'And I can make it even bigger.'

Antoinette laughed her loud laugh. 'How big?' she teased.

'Like I said, as big as you want.'

'I'm intrigued. What do you have in mind?' she asked.

'It's more like whether you want to toy with your mind,' he retaliated.

There was an instant's silence – an instant in which everything altered. Antoinette's laughter deflated like a balloon suddenly gasping for air.

'I don't do drugs,' she said.

'I think you should,' Jason replied.

*

Seven hours later, an early-morning riser's brisk walk had come to an abrupt stop. He scratched his head, wondering about the car he'd come across in a ditch just off the main road. He carefully opened the sedan's front door, wondering if someone might be in need of help.

'Nobody inside,' he muttered minutes later, 'nothing except a blood-red kaftan.'

# Table for Four

'We should invite Miss Pelly to tea,' Nan said, smiling.

So we did.

Nan and I had spent many a pleasurable hour of my school holidays together watching Miss Pelly, as we'd nicknamed her, glide above the big, leafy backyard of Nan's home.

'It's as if she's putting on a show – just for us,' I remember telling Nan the first time I saw the pelican glide, then spread her ample black and white-tinged wings as if in greeting, flying back and forth, back and forth, mesmerising us with the stylish splendour of her form.

'Isn't she gorgeous?' said Nan. 'I love the distinct pink of her bill.'

'Wonder why she's on her own?' I asked.

'Always has been, ever since I first saw her.'

'Do you remember when that was?' I asked.

'Oh…about the same time you were born.'

I'd just turned fourteen, and I'd been coming to Nan's home ever since I could remember – once a year, during the December holidays. As far as I could tell, Miss Pelly was a frequent visitor.

There was a reason, of course, that Miss Pelly loved Nan's home. My grandmother had a gentle, but consistently flowing, stream in her backyard – and it had been forever stocked with fish, just the kind Miss Pelly loved.

It was surprising for her species of bird that Miss Pelly had always been on her own. It was as if Nan's home was Miss Pelly's secret hideaway, her Cinderella place, the place she could always come to, where she felt safe and secure, where she fitted perfectly, like a foot in a snug shoe.

And where she would always be fed, as the solo fly-in, fly-out visitor.

*

The day that changed was one Nan and I would never forget. I remember Nan calling for me urgently.

'Rebekah, Rebekah, darling…come and see.'

I dashed from my bed, surprised by the earnestness in Nan's voice. She was normally as composed as all sensible grandmothers in the face of a crisis.

'What is it, Nan?' I said, rubbing my eyes as I entered the garden.

'It's Miss Pelly – come out here quickly.'

Fearing the worst, I did as Nan asked.

'Look, look up there.'

I glanced up, using an arm to protect my eyes from the sun.

'She's got a companion,' Nan pointed out.

As I focused, I saw Miss Pelly accompanied by a mirror image of her – except it was a miniature version.

'She must have been with little one,' said Nan. 'Now I know why she's been looking more podgy than usual.'

That was when Nan issued her unusual invitation. 'We should invite Miss Pelly to tea,' she said, adding, 'both of them, Mum and her baby…'

*

So, next morning, we set a table outside, near the stream. I helped Nan arrange the plates. We placed a slice of her home-made carrot cake on each of ours. On one of the remaining two plates, Nan arranged a large perch she'd hooked from the stream earlier that morning. On the smaller of the two plates, she placed two sardines.

'Do you think they'll come?' I asked Nan.

'She's trusted us for years – no reason she'd change now.'

We sat, prepared to be patient, but it would not be for long. On cue, Miss Pelly flew overhead, accompanied by the newcomer, trying with some difficulty to emulate her mother's effortless, gracious glide.

Just then, the doorbell rang.

'I'll get it, Nan,' I said, dashing to see who our unexpected visitor might be. It was a stranger, asking for directions which I gave as hurriedly as I could. Slightly miffed by the intrusion, I rushed back outside.

Nan sat quietly. A look of content covered her face, the kind you have after finishing a sumptuous meal. 'They came for tea,' she whispered.

I glanced at the table. The two slices of carrot cake remained untouched. The giant perch was gone. So were the two sardines.

I looked up, trying to see where they were.

'Look there,' said Nan, pointing at the ground.

In the sand, two pairs of webbed prints – one larger pair, the other much smaller – led from the tea table down to the stream.

'I missed them, Nan, I missed them,' I cried in dismay. 'That silly man made me miss them.'

Nan was unmoved. 'Don't worry, darling,' she said, calmly, 'I promise you – they'll be back.'

# On the Road to Somewhere

Jack Smith was a loner. He'd been that way most of his life. It was why he'd never wed. He loved women. They adored him. But he couldn't stomach being restricted to a life of marriage, to one woman, for ever. So he'd chosen to remain on his own, even though there was one thing he craved. The yearning was greater than the need for women, the beers, the freedom even.

It was a son. He'd always wished to bond with a son, a son he could cherish.

Jack had always been a complex individual. Opportunities often arose for him, but he was too respectful of women. He'd promised himself he would never exploit a woman's love for him, just to realise his dream for a child. As usual, though, this meant fleeing another relationship which had become serious. This time, he knew, like fishermen just know how to hook a barramundi, he had to head north.

Days later, Jack Smith hopped on a train to Darwin.

*

Jack had travelled through most of Australia, leaving scores of relationships behind him. One positive out of the termination of loving partnerships, the amazing women he'd met, the heartache, was that he'd travelled far and wide to ensure the physical distance from someone who'd fallen for him.

Jack was fortunate he'd come into some money via his maternal grandparents, who'd died within months of each other. They had also been his parents, legally adopting him when his single mum had deserted him, just like his father had done years before.

Probably why I can't hack this relationship business, he thought again. My dad just upped and left me, my mum did the same. They couldn't stay with each other, and neither of them could stay with me.

Though his grandparents were kind – God knows how he would've turned out if they hadn't been around – he'd always felt like he was a noose around their necks. He'd helped with chores on their smallholding and loved the solitude of the outback town in which they lived. He'd sought solace in Nature and it wasn't surprising he'd ended up working as a shearer.

'Time to see the world,' he'd told his grandfather of his decision to leave permanently.

'Always work around here, son,' his grandfather had replied.

'Nah…got itchy feet, Pa – have to move on.'

He'd felt guilty about leaving. He'd ditched them at a time when they were starting to need help. When he'd heard news of their deaths, he'd felt bad. He'd felt worse when he'd heard they'd left what they had to him, even though there were other grandchildren.

Don't go there again, Jack told himself on the Darwin-bound train. I'm heading north for a reason, he reasoned, though he had no idea what that was.

*

Jack was lulled from his snooze by the urgency of a woman's voice. It came from the seat just two rows in front of him.

'Why?' asked the woman's female companion.

'I don't want this baby any more.'

'You're not serious, Maggie.'

'I am serious. I know I'll hate him. I hate his father. So, I'll hate him too.'

The woman named Maggie blew her nose into the hanky she clutched as tightly as a toddler clasps a lolly.

Jack could see she was young. Despite himself, he continued listening.

'But, Maggie, you've already come this far with the child.'

'I don't care – I've been given the name of a guy who can help me…'

'But how do you know he's legit?'

'I don't. But either I do this or I kill myself and the kid when he's born.'

Jack saw Maggie lower her head – and sob again into the hanky, already as soggy as a baby's nappy. He wondered if he should intervene, offer advice. Then he wondered where that had come from. What advice would he have that could change her situation?

'Nah – leave them to it, none of my business,' he told himself.

*

She can't do it, Jack thought. I won't let her do it.

As passengers alighted the train in Darwin three hours later, Jack approached the woman who'd sat in the seat two rows from him, the woman named Maggie.

Jack knew what he was about to do could salvage her life. He knew for sure, it would cause a momentum shift in his.

''Scuse me, love,' he said.

'What?' the woman reacted, angered at the stranger's intrusion.

Jack spoke firmly, 'I want you to have that baby.'

'What the hell?' she shrieked. 'Who are you? What are you saying?'

Jack was not one to cower. He engaged the woman's eyes, unwavering in their directness. As lightly as a whisper, he told her, 'I want you to have that baby – because I want to adopt him.'

# Break From Reality

Simona went to her enchanted place often. It was her relief, her escape from her crazy life. It was somewhere she went when living got too much for her, when they got too much for her…her childlike husband, his parents, her parents, her two young children. When it all got too much for her, she went to her enchanted place, where there were no worries, no problems, no dilemmas…just fond memories.

*

Ten deep breaths were all Simona needed to be on her way. They were very deep breaths. Breathe in to a count of five, breathe out to a count of five, breathe in, breathe out…soon she was at the entrance: the rose-red door on the top of the cliff, the rose-red door with the eucalypt-green door handle. She placed her hand on the handle of the door, turned it to her right, and walked through, closing the rose-red door on the other side after turning the eucalypt-green handle, and securing the latch. She had taken the first steps to her enchanted place.

*

Simona looked over the cliff, then out to sea. It was a long way down but that was never a problem. She always carried her wings with her. She called them her angel wings. They would take her to her enchanted place, the place where her childlike husband, his parents, her parents and her two young children would never find her. She attached the wings, no bigger than those of a young, soaring eagle – though her wings were white – and flew to her enchanted place, her tiny island in the ocean.

*

Within seconds of landing, Simona felt the stress wash from her. On the island – a section of rock jutting out from the ocean's depth – Simona breathed in the sea air. Five deep breaths in, five deep breaths out… it's special, that smell of the ocean, she thought. A mix of seaweed, salt and air – a concoction made in heaven. She stayed with the aroma even after the deep in-out breaths…

*

Then the sounds stirred her…the sounds of gulls, pelicans and other bird life, gently jostling for room on the overpopulated rock; a wispy wind valiantly attempting to make its voice heard above bird chatter; the greeting of a delighted dolphin lolling on the periphery; the din of waves crashing against the rock. Thankfully, she thought, Nature's eloquence easily drowned out any attempts of verbal interference in her headspace.

*

Simona looked out from her enchanted place, the place she also called her hidey-hole in the sea…she saw aeroplanes overhead; boats being launched; children and dogs running across the wet sand, the dry sand…but these human escapades were overwhelmed by what she really focused upon…shapely hills draped in shadows and sunlight; a clear horizon break between the similar hues of sky and ocean; waves curling and crashing, always curling and crashing; the textures of the wet and dry shores; the sea birds; and the lone dolphin, laughing, smiling a smile as wide as the ocean, encouraging her to have another go…

*

The invitation was too hard to resist. Simona attached her wet suit, which stuck like a second skin to her body, and clambered over bits of jagged rock towards the dolphin. She patted his face with her bare hands, then jumped into a sea so chilly even her wetsuit seemed to draw a sharp intake of breath. She put her arms around the dolphin, feeling the warmth of its smooth skin, then, on his back, she strapped herself in. Soon they were diving in and out of waves, quickly hitting the depths, then shooting out of waves at breakneck speed. Exhilarating minutes went by in seconds as Simona become one with the dolphin, with the swells, with Nature…

*

Finally, she was back on her island. She unzipped the wetsuit, inviting the sun to embrace her. She licked the salt from around her mouth, guzzled a litre of fresh water, then a healthy mix of squeezed carrot, beetroot and celery juice. She settled into her beach chair, and sipped, leisurely, the nutty-flavoured coffee from the flask…focusing particularly upon the sights and then, with eyes firmly shut, the sounds, allowing them to envelop her in a warm cuddle.

*

Simona knew time in her enchanted place was close to being over. Regrettably, it was time to depart. She had to retrace her steps. She waved farewell to Nature, attached her wings, flew back to the top of the cliff, walked through the rose-red door with the eucalypt-green door handle, closed and latched it behind her, and took ten deep breaths, with a count of five inwards and, another count of five, outwards; inwards, outwards…

*

Simona smiled. It was a smile which signalled contentment, peace of mind. She was ready again to face the world, ready to face her childlike husband, his parents, her parents and her two young children. All it had taken was ten minutes – ten minutes of meditation that was out of this world.

45

# Place of Darkness

Usually, at night, in the place Joshua and his mother lived, the wind sounded like a mad dog barking. The night the crash occurred, the wind sounded much more menacing.

Neither Joshua, nor his mother, had expected the tragedy. There had been three of them in the family then. It was Christmas, Joshua recalled. He remembered because, though they were poor, they always had their Christmas tree, with its tiny, flickering lights, and other decorations to brighten their lives.

Joshua's mother had always put up the tree on 1 December and put it away again on 31 December. It was the way her family, and her families before her, always did it.

Until the evening the accident occurred.

*

It was just a few nights before Christmas when Joshua's mother got the call.

Joshua knew before the phone hit the floor and smashed on to the concrete that the news wasn't good. His mother's hands had rushed up to her face quicker than death strikes. Her eyes were as wide as the pumpkins that grew, despite the drought, in their little vegetable garden out the back of the ordinary weatherboard they'd rented since Joshua had been born, fourteen years ago. Before his mother's thin legs collapsed under her and she fell to the concrete, clutching, then tearing at her thin, black hair she'd trimmed herself just that morning, he already knew. The wailing that came from his mother's mouth, way more horrible than the barking wind, confirmed for Joshua what his mother eventually screamed.

'He's dead, Joshua. Your father's truck rolled – he's dead.'

*

After the calamity, the Christmas tree stayed in the lounge room. Its flickering lights, like miniature versions of a lighthouse, always stayed on at night.

'Your father was alive when the tree was put up. It will stay up, with the lights flickering at night forever, while I'm alive,' his mother told Joshua.

His mother was traumatised beyond help. Days and nights, she remained in their small home, refusing to see anyone, even the local pastor who came knocking after a church service one Sunday to see if he could help.

'Tell him to go away,' his mother told Joshua. 'His God did this to our family – I don't want his help.'

During the day, Joshua's mother lay between the four walls of her tiny, windowless bedroom, a miniature photo of her wedding day clutched to her breast. Only at night, after she'd switched on the flickering lights on the Christmas tree, did she get up to cook a sparse meal for herself and Joshua.

The young boy's life was different, too, after his father's death. He'd left school and, when he could, tended to the vegetable garden so his mother had something to cook for their evening meal.

He found a job at the local deli to help pay the rent, which had been reduced, thanks to their sympathetic landlord. He had no relatives and no friends. In any case, there was little time for either. He was now the head of the house. He knew it was only his care that kept his mother alive.

Often he wondered whether she'd be at home when he got back from work as the tentacles of dusk devoured the house. Or if she might have packed a bag, and set off into the bush, to find another life somewhere else.

He questioned her about it one night.

'I live only for you, Joshua – and the Christmas lights,' was her reply. Joshua was strangely assured by that.

*

His mother's pledge appeared to unravel the night he was forced to work later than usual. Locals in the town had been pre-warned of a storm about to hit the next day. The deli had been invaded by mums and dads stocking up, just in case.

The wild wind tore at Joshua, now sixteen, as he wheeled his way from the town's centre to his home, ten kilometres away. He was fortunate the gale was behind him, enabling him to freewheel part of the way. Still, his bicycle was hard to control and passing trucks drove perilously close to the fast-pedalling figure.

By the time Joshua arrived home, darkness, as sombre as a graveyard at midnight, had set in. About to insert the front-door key, Joshua faltered. He peered through the lounge-room window.

Then, as had happened to his mother two years before, his legs gave way, this time on the outside porch. When he'd revived, the bleak blackness from within the house struck him with the force of a tornado.

For the first time since his father's death, the Christmas lights, those tiny, yet precious, beacons of brightness and hope night after night after night, were not flickering to greet him.

# Thanks for the Memories

'I love you, Cyril,' Gladys whispered.

'I love you too, Gladys,' Cyril sighed back.

It was time, they both knew, to become martyrs for their country's cause, for all those who loved them as the choice of treat on that special day of the year. Very soon, it would all be over for them, but they both knew their lives had been enriched by their chance meeting in the wilds of north America.

*

A year ago, they were on the run, the original Bonnie and Clyde. The pilgrims were out to get them, but the young couple, frisky and fleet-footed, wasn't ready to give in just then.

Cyril and Gladys had kept ahead of their chasing foes for many days. On the ground in the dense forest, they'd darted in and around prickly bushes and large trees at up to thirty kilometres an hour, evading the chasing mob with cunning. Their crimson wattles bobbed this way and that as if they were fanning themselves from the intense heat.

Now and again, too, they would rise to new heights.

'Lucky we can fly,' said Cyril.

'Yes, very lucky we're wild – not like those domestics,' replied Gladys.

As they soared higher, they could hear language as blue as the clear skies from the frustrated pilgrims below. They stayed close, careful to fly near canopy tops, which helped to keep them camouflaged.

Well clear now of their intended captors, the two settled quietly in a lush pasture for the night.

'It's all Ben's fault,' said Cyril.

'Ben?' asked Gladys.

'You know – Benjamin Franklin,' said Cyril.

'What exactly do you mean, dear?' Gladys asked.

Cyril chose to enlighten his darling Gladys. 'If Ben hadn't decided turkey would be more suited to Thanksgiving celebrations than everyone's favourite – the bald eagle – we wouldn't be in this pickle.'

'True,' said Gladys. 'But, even if I say so myself, I'd much prefer a turkey to celebrate our country's important day.'

Cyril lifted one eyelid, then both, as Gladys continued. 'Stuffed with that bread-based mixture, add a touch of sage – oh, what a herb! – chopped celery, carrot and onion, then all crisply roasted. Yum, yum, yum!'

Cyril was shocked. 'Horrible thought, Gladys – that's like giving cannibalism the thumbs-up.'

'Beats the heck out of pumpkin pie any time as dish of the day,' she said, impish as ever.

'You can be a little devil sometimes,' Cyril said.

At her gabbling best, there was no stopping Gladys. 'Just the thought of sucking on that wishbone from the breast of the plumpest turkey in town to cap off a great meal drives me dizzy with delight.'

'Gladys!' cried Cyril.

'Oh, lighten up, sweetheart.' Gladys grinned from jowl to jowl.

The sight of that smile made Cyril's heart beat ever so fast. His neck enlarged with the rush of blood, such was his excitement. That was a memorable moment for Cyril, the moment he realised how lucky he was to have shared his life with a partner like Gladys.

*

It was because they were no longer as nimble that Cyril and Gladys had come to the end of what for them had been an exciting adventure. They'd walked, run and flown for so long together – and snacked on so many delicious delicacies, including their favourite nuts and berries – that it was inevitable that their portly statures would eventually lead to their capture.

For many days and nights, they'd enjoyed the good life. Now they were going to provide a taste of the good life to at least two American families.

They accepted their fate without remorse. It was time to give.

Held down on adjacent chopping blocks, they whispered their love for each other, then gazed, with contentment, into each other's eyes.

And Cyril was sure he saw his beloved Gladys wink wickedly in his direction just a second or two before they both heard the cry, 'Off with their heads!'

# Stranger in the Mist

The kids thought he was mad. So did all the locals. I wasn't so sure.

*

We'd moved to Scarletville three years ago, soon after the divorce came through. I'd had enough of the life with Ed and his mood swings. The day he punched me in the face was the day I moved out. And filed for divorce.

Just weeks after moving out, the kids and I landed in Scarletville, a remote town in South Australia. Ed never bothered to find us. He loathed the kids as much as he hated me. I relocated to get a fresh start, away from his bashings, away from that life.

It had been a good move. I settled into a part-time job, the kids joyed the small local school, and I loved my rented home over-looking the beach. Everything was as perfect as it could be for a divorced mum always prepared to take risks.

I was grateful for my new life.

Only one thing bothered me. It was the weirdo, as the kids called him.

*

The first time I noticed the man was soon after we'd moved into our beach home. I saw him from my bedroom window, which faced the sea. He appeared from nowhere, like the gorilla out of the mist in that famous animal movie.

I watched him regularly during the winter months, early in the morning, when the mist danced in off the sea. By then, I'd taken to using my binoculars. I saw him clearly, as the haze cleared, on a few occasions.

He was of medium height and well-built, with a posture as straight as a ruler. His salt-and-pepper beard was unruly and flowed untidily from sun-bleached, curly hair. Bushy eyebrows framed a wrinkled face. I imagined he'd have eyes of different colours, one light blue and the other light green, both luminous against his dark skin, and unblinking, always. Two other things stood out. He was always barefoot. He also wore a scarlet hoody, faded and overlong, down to his knees. It looked more like a cloak. He reminded me of Superman, just from another era.

*

Halfway through our third winter in Scarletville, I made the decision. It scared the kids.

'You can't,' said the youngest one.

'He'll kill you,' said the other.

But I'd made up my mind. I was going to follow the madman on a day I spotted him walking on the beach. I was going to find out where he lived – and introduce myself.

One of the strangest things about Scarletville, our pleasant and welcoming town, was that no one knew where this man lived. Apparently, he'd appeared from nowhere five years ago and had never spoken to a soul in the time he'd lived in the vicinity which was, as one person said, 'in the bush somewhere'. Obviously, he'd kept to himself and was self-sufficient as he'd never gone to the local deli to stock up with provisions.

'Stay away from him,' one local said. 'He's probably dangerous.'

'Anyone been knocked off around here in the past five years?' I asked.

'No, but there's always a first time,' came the response.

I'd been a do-gooder since the day I rescued a bird caught in a trap when I was just six. That character trait had never got me into trouble.

I admit, too, I'd always been a stickybeak. This was a chance to meet someone mysterious.

*

It wasn't hard to pick up his trail on the day I decided to follow him. The pathway, once in the bush, was obvious from trodden grass. Not surprisingly, it was quite a trek. He was determined to be as far away from the main track as possible.

Eventually, I came to a clearing. I kept my distance, for some time surveying the area from behind a bush. I took in the scene. There were chooks in a covered pen. A vegie garden, with plants, lay thriving. Behind it rested a hut, almost as small as a cubby house. Its sides were covered in mud. Sheets of rusted iron lay loosely on top.

I thought of my kids.

I wanted to run away. Quickly.

I found myself walking. Not away, but towards the entrance.

I knocked on the makeshift front door.

'Hello, anyone there?' I heard myself saying.

The sound echoed back. There was no reply.

I repeated the query. Again, no reply.

A voice in my head kept repeating, 'Get away.'

Instead, I pushed open the door. Slowly. Carefully.

I stood in the doorway.

My eyes grappled with the dim light. As they focused, I saw the outline on the bed – and recoiled in horror.

# Out of His Hands

It was a cold morning. Freezing, in fact. But that didn't deter Anthony Campbell from kicking a football with his best mate, Joseph. At only fourteen, Anthony was in the prime of his young life. Not many years a teenager, he was already at a crossroads – having to decide where his talents might best lie. His parents had put it to him that if he wanted to make the grade in wherever he wanted to be in future, he had to make a choice. Now.

Anthony was a talented footballer. From a very young age, he could banana-kick goals from any angle. That skill thrilled spectators, particularly his grandparents, who idolised him.

It helped that Anthony's father had been an AFL player.

Anthony also had the voice of Keats' nightingale. He'd made his mark in the school choir as their lead singer and his singing teacher told his parents he was destined for greatness. His grandparents agreed with that assumption, too.

It helped that Anthony's mother had been a touring soprano.

'I'm still young – why can't I keep doing both?' he asked his parents.

'If you want to be the real deal in either, you have to choose,' said his dad.

'But…'

'You've said you want to become the best, haven't you?' said his mum.

'Yes, but…'

'Well, you can't become the best if you're dividing your time,' said his dad.

'And we can't spare the time fetching and carrying you every day of the week,' said his mum. 'We have other kids to consider too.'

So the boy who would be a star had to decide. Sooner rather than later.

Anthony had many other plusses, aside from his obvious skills. Charming, good-looking in a country-boy kind of way, he had a mischievous smile which endeared him to everyone, particularly older people such as his grandparents. He was also a positive role model. But, just the same as everyone else in the world, he was imperfect. He had the annoying mannerism of flicking back his long, black hair with a jerk of his head.

'Just like that little sod, Justin whatshisname,' said his grandmother.

Anthony was also indecisive – which made the choice between footy and singing so difficult to make.

*

'What should I do?' he asked Joseph, the best mate who'd been invited on a trip away with Anthony and his parents. They'd decided to go on a long weekend venture – three days which would decide the boy's fate.

'Do what your heart tells you,' said Joseph.

'But I love footy and singing equally,' said Anthony.

'You've gotta decide,' said Joseph.

'I know, but it's too hard,' said Anthony, with a jerk of his head.

'Then let fate decide for you.'

'Whadya mean?'

'You'll see,' said Joseph.

Anthony didn't see, but trusted his mate's instincts.

So it proved.

On the final day of another wintry morning, while the boys were out alone, Anthony fell down a cliff, dislocating his left leg. Very badly. So seriously that specialists unanimously concluded any sporting career involving body contact would never be a possibility for Anthony.

*

Two years later, a group of performers took to the stage yet again to re-ceive the accolades of another appreciative audience.

Anthony Campbell took centre stage as the leading light in the world-renowned Kookaburras travelling choir. The choir was on the last leg of the tour, which had been on the road for more than three months, travelling around Australia, North America and Europe.

Rapturous applause had greeted each sold-out performance – Anthony, in particular, thrilling audiences with a voice Mario Lanza would have envied and a disarming personality even that maddening hair-flick could not sabotage.

As he bowed in another encore, Anthony thought back to when he'd reached the crossroads of his life two years back – and smiled broadly that the decision he'd had to make had been taken out of his hands, just as his friend, Joseph, had predicted.

As light snow fell on the Swiss Alps, on the morning after the night before, Anthony kicked a footy with his mate and his father on the white-covered lawn of their holiday home, and decided his life could not be any happier.

He'd been blessed with good genes – and when his body had let him down, he'd become a star in a profession ultimately made for him.

And, like all knowing mothers, his mum, the ex-soprano star who watched the trio from inside their toasty home, cupped her hands around a mug of hot cocoa on that freezing morning, and murmured to herself, 'I always knew he'd choose singing.'

# Decision Time

Peter Thomas. An ordinary name for a seemingly ordinary bloke. And Peter did look run-of-the-mill. Of medium build, he had mousy brown hair and beige eyes to go with a body so pale anyone would think he never saw the sun. Always top of his maths and science classes, Peter preferred his own company. He had no friends, and always sat in the front row of his classes – on his own. He chose to ignore everyone else's business. His theory was if he did that, there was no chance of becoming involved. If he saw something he didn't like, he'd wipe it from his mind. He was a loner and he was determined to keep it that way, regardless of consequences.

He was definitely strange. That's why fingers would point his way when they found the body in the toilet block.

*

Peter Thomas was anxious. Not surprisingly. He knew once the story got out about the body in the toilet block, he'd be a prime suspect. So, he had to get rid of the bag. Not many students carried a thirty-centimetre-long screwdriver in a school bag. Especially an implement sharp enough to cut through the thickest of lamb chops. So Peter knew he'd have to get rid of it. No one would believe the real reason he carried the screwdriver and he was not keen to test this theory on anyone right now.

Peter knew he was a little weird compared with most kids in his class. He was nothing like Jason Knight, the jock, thick as the school-yard's dead tree trunk, but still able to reel in the girls as easily as collecting a bite in a lake full of salmon. Said more about the girls than about Jason, Peter always thought.

Neither was Peter anything like Spratty, the school's famous nerd, known only by his nickname. Only high-tech electronics interested Spratty, and he didn't care that he always dressed in a T-shirt, long shorts, sandals and long, white socks. One look at Spratty and it was obvious girls were the last thing on his mind.

Peter, on the other hand, though a solitary figure, and a maths and science genius, liked girls. A lot. And there was one girl especially who caught his eye. Not only was Rosanne Newberry smart (she always finished just behind him in maths and science exams) but she was gorgeous, too. At least Peter thought so. It was true she loved colour but it didn't concern Peter that Rosanne dressed as brightly as her IQ. He liked that about her. Or, at least, he did.

Peter knew it was Rosanne's body that had been found in the toilet block. He also thought he knew why she'd been killed.

*

'So, why'd you do it, mate?' The detective was questioning Peter Thomas. 'You know she was slit from throat to stomach with a sharp instrument.'

'Wasn't me,' replied Peter.

The detective wasn't in the mood to muck around. 'What about the screwdriver in your school bag, then?'

Peter's pale face turned red as blood. He was angry with himself. He should have dumped the bag. But, as usual, he was too slow. Quick at summing up maths answers and as swift on the uptake at science experiments, he always lagged in the ordinary, day-to-day things people did. That was in his nature. It was, unfortunately, what usually got him into trouble.

'Well?' the detective persisted.

Peter knew scrutiny of the screwdriver would clear him. 'You're welcome to check it out,' he told the detective.

'We already have, but that doesn't mean you didn't have time to clean it up.'

Peter wasn't interested in games. However, he knew if he didn't tell the truth, he'd continue to be a suspect. 'I use it for myself – on myself,' he told the detective.

'What do you mean?'

Peter blushed again. 'I clean my teeth with it,' he admitted, looking away.

'Thought you were odd, but not that loony.' The detective wasn't smiling. 'So who do you think did it?'

'That's your job, detective, not mine.'

*

Peter Thomas might have been a strange boy. But it didn't take him long to work things out. Things that were important, like the killing of the only girl in school he liked. And he knew something the detective obviously didn't.

He knew the only girl in the school that big-headed jock, Jason Knight, was unable to lay his hands on, despite his persistence, was Rosanne Newberry, the girl who now lay dead.

Peter, the strange boy who never got involved in anyone else's business, also knew the last time he'd seen Jason Knight, he'd been running away from the toilet block with a bright orange bandana hanging out from a trouser pocket.

Peter also was certain that bandana would have belonged to only one girl.

# Alice's Wonderful Lesson

Alice was loving Wonderland. She'd met so many interesting creatures, most of whom had weird and wonderful personalities.

She certainly liked the white rabbit. After all, it was he who'd led her to this unearthly place. He was very gentlemanly, breaking her fall as she tumbled down the rabbit hole which was almost as long as a ball of string. Sweet and gentle soul he was, Alice thought, appearing at various times throughout her stay just when she needed him. Even though the poor thing never seemed to know what time it was.

She also favoured the Cheshire cat. Alice called him Smiley. He was a funny character, who seemed to disappear, then reappear at will. Sometimes, he even vanished but forgot to take his huge grin with him. In some ways, Alice was convinced, Smiley would remind her about the time in her life between childhood and adulthood. Alice couldn't recall exactly what that was called.

One person she didn't like much was the Queen of Hearts. Alice thought her a tyrant, a word she'd learned just before arriving in Wonderland. If the queen didn't get her way, she became quite mad. As Alice grew wiser during her adventure in Wonderland, the queen became even madder, almost as crazy as the Mad Hatter.

But Alice's two favourite characters were, of course, the ones who stole the show on her Big Night Out: the caterpillar and the March hare, who hosted the Mad Hatter's Tea Party. Of course, it wasn't really one very special night because, as was well known, the tea party was a never-ending event.

To Alice, though, this night was going to be a big one because she'd been invited to partner the caterpillar. The caterpillar was a wise man who didn't always seem to act wisely. He appeared to lead little people astray – not in a horrible way, but in a way that encouraged them to try things they should not. The caterpillar, as was well known, was always helpful to Alice by telling her she could eat portions of mushrooms if she wanted to get taller or smaller.

'Why would I want to do that, Mr Caterpillar?' asked Alice.

'Well, sometimes you need to be small to get into nooks and crannies around Wonderland,' said the caterpillar. 'And, other times, if you need to throw your weight around, when you want to put the nasty queen in her place, then it's good to have a slice of mushroom – and grow bigger.'

Alice nodded. 'It must be smashing to be so wise,' she told him.

The caterpillar nodded back. And smiled, which he didn't do very often. Guess we all like compliments, thought Alice.

On the big night, the caterpillar escorted Alice to the Mad Hatter's Tea Party. Alice had dressed in cheerful colours, because she wanted to look like all the other odd characters at the party.

She greeted everyone with a smile as wide as half a watermelon. Though she was a stranger to some, they all welcomed her as if she'd always lived in Wonderland.

Halfway through the night, the caterpillar told Alice to do something she really shouldn't do. He wanted Alice to smoke his hookah, which he was now doing, while sitting atop a mushroom, which he sometimes took bites of, too.

Alice wondered if it was a good idea. She remembered that a drug lurked inside the hookah. And chewing on a magic mushroom at the same time also worried her. 'I don't think I should smoke that,' Alice told the caterpillar.

'It won't do you any harm,' he said. 'I've been smoking it for most of my life, and I'm fine.'

'I'm only nine,' said Alice. 'My mum and dad in the real world wouldn't be happy if they knew I was smoking already.'

'I won't tell if you don't,' said the caterpillar.

'Well, I won't tell them – because I'm not going to try it!' said Alice, stamping her feet.

The caterpillar whooped with delight at Alice's response. 'Good on you, Alice,' he said. 'It was just a test. If you had put that hookah to your mouth, I would have handed you over to the nasty Queen of Tarts…sorry, Hearts…to punish you. Thank heaven I didn't have to do that.' The caterpillar gave Alice a friendly hug and, still smoking his hookah, crawled away in his squiggly fashion.

While Alice did not have time in this tale to chatter about the March hare, it was safe to say Alice was happy in Wonderland. She was pleased all the characters she'd met so far had taught her something about life and growing up in a dangerous world.

She knew that when she finally left Wonderland, she would help write a book – and perhaps even be a character in it. The book would be read by millions of girls and boys, who would learn lessons about life, just like the one she'd learned about not giving in to temptation on a big night out.

# Storm in a Teacup

Jake whistled, nonchalant as you like, as she walked past.

'Shallow bastard,' Simone yelled, flicking a middle finger in his direction.

Jake roared in delight. 'You'd thank your lucky stars if you were going on a date with me,' he shouted.

Simone paused, retraced her steps and faced the man she put at the head of her jerk inventory. 'I'd love to dislocate one of your limbs,' she told Jake. 'And stick it up the part of your body where the sun seldom shines.'

'C'mon, Simone, you know you're top of my dating pool,' Jake responded.

'Listen, mate, you don't do it for me,' said Simone. 'I prefer my men with brains. And, busy. Not a layabout like you.' She wasn't quite done. 'You're way down the list of blokes I'd want to hook up with, so get that through your thick skull, buddy.'

Jake was never one to take insults without a comeback. 'Honey, sweetheart, cutie,' he said. 'Here's a little warning: prepare to fall in love.'

Simone was as fiery as a dry bush blaze. It was one of the things about her that attracted Jake. 'No hope in hell that'll happen, mate,' she replied. 'I know too much about you – you and your roving eye.'

'Been to the library to check my credentials, have you?' asked Jake.

'I'd need the archives to find stuff on you, you old perve,' Simone said.

Jake was ten years older than Simone, newly out of her teenage years. He knew he was on to a hiding in the age debate.

'OK, I give up,' said Jake. 'I suggest we hit the pub for some cool air. You're not the only thing out here that's hot. I'll even stand you a gin and tonic.'

'Stick it up yer bum, mate,' Simone yelled back, swinging her ample hips loudly as she walked away, brisk as you like.

*

Jake spent a fruitless fortnight trying to decide what needed to be done to persuade Simone to accompany him on a night out. Once I've given her the full treatment, like all the others, she'll find me too hard to resist, he eventually assured himself.

He dialled her number. They lived in a small town, so it had been easy to locate.

'Simone,' he said. 'It's your favourite fellow. You up for that date?'

'Not interested,' she responded.

'I'll do whatever you want,' he said.

There were moments of quiet. It was unusual for her.

'Simone? You there?'

'Shut up,' she said. 'Just thinking what I want that you can't give me.' She paused again. 'I've got it: a ride in a red convertible to a fancy restaurant. Your shout – for the lot.'

Jake didn't have a chance to respond.

'Pick me up at six on Saturday night,' added Simone, switching off her phone.

Jake smiled. He'd enticed her. His brain was already in overdrive, but he did, for a minute or two, wonder how he was going to get this done.

*

Jake always had used-car parts in his backyard – and front yard, too. He was clever at putting things together, so mates always dropped off scrap cars at his house. When he got the urge, which wasn't often, he'd use a bit of this or that to get wheels back on the road.

Jake got to work. It took quite a few days, and nights, to have a convertible up and running. It was blue, so he spray-painted it red. He borrowed a suit and bow tie from his best mate – and a loan from another acquaintance for a decent meal for two.

As he drove to Simone's home late Saturday afternoon, Jake was tempted to toot the car's horn all the way up the street. He decided instead to impress her with a rugged door-knock and a bunch of cheap blooms.

Simone was dressed in figure-hugging red. He knew his efforts would be worth it. He expected a happy ending.

'Not bad for a bludger,' was Simone's response to both his outfit and the car.

And she kept things close to her ample chest throughout a meal so expensive that Jake panicked he wouldn't have enough cash to pay for it.

'Good job for an old bloke,' said Simone as she sifted through the remains of her cuppa which concluded the meal. 'Must admit, it was bloody good tucker,' she told Jake, excited now about what the later evening held in store.

'But it's a one-off,' she added. 'And that's it, mate.'

'What? What do you mean?' said Jake.

'I mean this first date is our last – and it ends right here.'

'You cannot be serious,' said Jake. 'Why?'

'Well, if you really must know, I'm a believer – and you can't argue with them.'

'You're crazy, woman. Believe in what? Argue with who?'

'The leaves,' said Simone.

'The leaves?' Jake mimicked.

'Yep,' said Simone triumphantly. 'I've come to the end of my cuppa and the tea leaves are revealing that there's a storm brewing…which means you and I are gonski…see ya, loser. I'll find my own way home.'

# Retirement Blues

'It's in there,' she said.

'Where?' he asked again.

'Bottom drawer,' she said.

'I've looked. It's not,' he replied.

'You're looking with your willy again,' she said.

'Stale joke,' he replied. Then the tirade began. 'Look, I've gone through that drawer and found candles and matches, which to my way of thinking, shouldn't be there. Dishcloths and oven gloves, which should. Tubes of cling wraps, which I get, but…why the heck are there six pairs of chopsticks there? When did we last use them? We don't even use them in a Chinese restaurant any more.'

'You never know,' she said.

'Never know what? That half a dozen Chinese soccer players are going to appear on our front doorstep – and ask for a feed, as long they can eat with our chopsticks?'

Edgar was on another rant. And Marie was sick of her life.

Every day seemed to end the same way as the one before. Edgar was out of control, with every minor problem becoming as big as Brexit, Marie thought.

'I've looked in every bloody drawer,' Edgar yelled again. 'And I can't find my bottle opener anywhere. That's it! I'm going to the pub…you can have tea on your own.'

Marie heard the front door slam.

It was time for another visit.

*

Marie's psychologist was perturbed. 'We've got to find a way to break Edgar's pattern of negativity,' she told Marie. 'What appealed to you most when you first started going out with him?'

Marie had only recently started seeing a psychologist. She'd asked Edgar to attend sessions with her.

He'd refused before she'd even finished asking him. 'No ways I'm seeing a shrink,' he'd shouted. 'If you need one, you go!'

So she did. She'd been seeing the psychologist for a month before their chopsticks fracas. Marie had told her that their twenty years of marriage had been happy, generally. But since Edgar no longer worked and they were both at home, things had changed. Edgar had become snappy, rude and inconsiderate. He'd never been like that before he'd left work.

'Retirement blues,' the psychologist had told Marie, who'd giggled at the notion.

'I'm serious,' the specialist had said. 'Nine out of ten couples who've been married for twenty years or more suffer from this affliction when they both leave their working lives and suddenly have to live with each other full time.'

Marie had arched an eyebrow, then nodded. 'It makes sense,' she'd said.

'So you're not the only person in this boat,' the psychologist had said, with a wry smile, 'and I can see this research is already making you feel better.'

Over the initial sessions, Marie had told the psychologist about her marital woes. Today's session involved strategies.

'So what attracted you to Edgar when you first met?' the psychologist asked again.

'Well, he wasn't handsome nor physically attractive,' said Marie. 'But he had a sense of humour – and often made me chuckle. We laughed a lot during our early years of courting and marriage because I did things to make him grin too.'

'Bingo!' said the psychologist. 'Work on something that you think might make him laugh again – and see how you go.'

*

Marie had agonised over a plan for almost as long as she'd struggled for perfection in her Year 10 exams. Finally, she'd come up with an idea she thought, through Edgar's eyes, would score high marks.

It was Friday night, their usual evening out. She was waiting for Edgar to come home from his regular hour-long jog before they went for their weekly pub tea. He'd been calmer during the week, eventually apologising for his chopsticks outburst, even promising he'd make it up to her.

'I've got a surprise for you,' Marie said, when he arrived home. 'Not only did I find your bottle opener in the middle drawer, I also found something else tucked away in a plastic bag.'

Marie had practised the routine a number of times during the day and thought she had it down pat: with a quick flick of her wrist, the button on her skirt fell open to reveal undies…which weren't hers. They were her gran's favourite knickers…big, beige and shapeless. They fitted her the same way an oversized jumper alters a body in winter.

Edgar, still holding the bunch of roses he'd brought in, resembled a quivering paperclip as he bent over with laughter. 'That's pretty sexy,' he said, with an exaggerated roll of his eyes. 'We're on the same wavelength again, honey,' he said.

'What do you mean?' said Marie.

'Well, I've got a confession to make.'

'What is it?' said Marie, a little uneasy.

'I didn't go for a run just then.'

'Oh?' said Marie.

'No, I was at a novelty store instead, getting these…'

On cue, Edgar dropped his shorts, then did an awkward pirouette …in a revealing bright blue G-string.

# Why Me?

Mark Alonzo felt the blood seep from his face. He could not believe what he'd just heard.

'We find the accused guilty,' the head juror had announced to the court.

Mark realised he'd have to spend at least twenty years behind bars – for something he didn't do.

He couldn't kill a fly. He always remembered the summers on the farm when his mother gave him the swatter to slay flies which they both knew would be first to try to tuck into the roast she'd slavishly cooked. He'd go around pretending to kill, but deliberately missing. He was that kind of child.

Nothing had changed in subsequent years. He couldn't harm a fly. Yet now he was guilty of killing a human being.

He looked at his daughter, Annie. So young. There was a chance this could be the last time he'd see her. His wife, her mother, was dead. There was little chance his mother-in-law, now Annie's custodian, would allow his daughter to visit him. He couldn't stomach that.

As the judge gave the call for the court to rise, Mark Alonzo bent down to pull out the blade of a paring knife buried in the sole of his shoe...

*

Mark had re-met his future wife, Sarah, many years ago, in a pub. That was no surprise. It was the place where most young people in the country town had gathered. Particularly if they were looking for a partner. And Mark was. He was thirty-two and knew he needed someone special in his life – someone who'd look after him, someone with whom he could share his life's memories and secrets, someone with whom he could start a family.

Mark had been looking for some time. He'd been a regular at the Vic, as the pub was called, during that time. Most people he'd met during that period were acquaintances rather than friends. Mark was a bit of a loner. He'd only frequent the pub for a couple of beers – mainly to check if there were newcomers, perhaps someone who'd steal his heart.

The day Sarah arrived was when his world became a different place.

'G'day stranger,' Mark heard the stunning blonde say as he'd walked into the pub after a long stint in the bush.

He'd been mustering cattle for most of the week, a slog tough enough to warrant a few coldies. 'Talking to me?' he grinned at the blonde.

'Yes, Mark, I am,' she said.

Mark smiled. He had deep dimples either side of a playful grin. They appealed to women. He had no idea, however, who *this* woman was.

'Heard you were a regular at the Vic,' said the blonde. 'Now that I'm back in town, thought I'd pop in to say g'day.'

'Okay, okay…' said Mark, 'it looks like you're not going to come to my rescue with a name, so I'll have to have a closer look…if that's okay with you.'

'Go for it,' she said, looking up at him like a child smugly hiding her best ever secret.

He put both hands into his pockets in case they decided to place themselves somewhere they shouldn't. He got up close.

'Still no idea?' she said, laughing now at Mark's discomfort.

'You're not…you're not…Sarah Rinaldi? Sarah, is that you? Is that really you?'

Swiftly, his hands escaped his pockets and clasped instead around a waist which wasn't much wider than it was when the pair were sweethearts for much of their later primary school years. He twirled her round and round, not wanting to let go, realising instantly this was why he was never able to get close to another woman for the past twelve years.

'What are you doing back here?' he yelled, still twirling her.

Sarah filled in the gaps since her departure when she and her parents had left their country town so she could attend senior school and later university in the Big Smoke. Sarah had studied to become a teacher. She'd then moved to other parts of Australia to widen her experience. Understandably, they'd lost contact. Now she'd returned to teach at the local school they'd both attended as young students.

It wasn't long before their juvenile passion rekindled. They'd married, had a lovely daughter, and lived a happy life.

At least it was – until the day Sarah's body was found in a shallow grave down the side of the big farm shed, a few days after she'd disappeared. A rare ugly stoush between the pair was overheard by a visiting tourist to their farm – and this proved to be a crucial detail in the case against the devastated farmer.

*

As Mark Alonzo bent down to pull out the weapon concealed in his shoe after being found guilty of his wife's murder, court officials rushed towards him. Mark took a fleeting glance at his beautiful daughter – and lifted the blade.

# In My Oasis

I'm the ladybird who lives in a forest in suburbia. It feels like a forest, probably because I'm tiny but, really, it's probably because the owners of the house just love to make their backyard especially green. Sometimes I feel it's my special oasis and that they put it together just for me and all my other ladybird friends.

I have to share my backyard with other insects and creatures, of course. But I don't mind, as long as they're friendly.

I don't mind Larry the Lizard 'cos he mostly lingers all day on the lounger, as you might find out later in this collection of tales.

Nor do I mind the cabbage white butterfly caterpillars who snack on the garden vegies, though the owners don't fancy them because they think they're a bit greedy.

The bees, of course, are really noisy, particularly when the blooms are dripping with nectar as tasty as honey from a hive. They're big talk really – I reckon their buzzing is way worse than their stings.

We also had Fergie the Frog visit for a couple of nights. He croaked a lot, particularly when the days drew to their close and the evening stars presented themselves as fireflies against the murky background. He annoyed all of us. I could tell the owners weren't happy with Fergie. They hunted him down after two sleepless nights and I saw him disappear down a drain – the one through which he came up. Thankfully, he hasn't been back. Touch wood!

I should have introduced you earlier to the owners of my property. There's only one I'm really fond of. She's the lady of the house who, as is often the case these days, seems to do everything around the home. Not only has she created my enchanting forest, she's also always fixing everything, inside and out. Mrs Fixit I call her. Lovely, lovely lady. I reckon he, that's her hubby, batted right out of his league when he started courting her. Sadly, she fell for his charm. Silly girl. Could have done so much better.

Mrs Fixit, as I've said, has created this wonderful oasis while he sits in his office, pretending to be a writer. Occasionally, he'll come out to the garden and trim the stamp-sized grassed area with a push lawn-mower. What a whinger!

His other job is to clean up the spoils left behind by their lovely dog, Luckie. Not sure why they call him that. Or spell it that way. I reckon Mr Hubby should be called Luckie, but I digress…

I was going to take you on a tour of this splendid backyard they've created for me and my other ladybird friends who visit often. So come on in…

On their side of the boundary line are hedges of softly waving bamboo. They hide the bland colourbond fence very cleverly.

There's a comfy lime lounge suite which provides another shade of green, and there's a large dining table with eight chairs for their many family dinners. I could tell you stories about some of their get-togethers. Perhaps it's better I don't.

Of course, in the backyard there are the mandatory water tanks and a washing line, positioned so they're not noticeable.

My home owners also have a secluded outside shower for when Mr Hubby comes back from his swims in the sea. He showers in the nuddy sometimes which is not a sight to behold, particularly for my ladybird friends, who always blush a brighter shade of red when that happens.

Also in the backyard space is a fishpond with fountain, and flowers and plants of many kinds; a herb garden with all Mrs Fixit's favourites (basil is my favourite); a vegie garden as mentioned, lush and always manure-smelly; and grapevines, lavender bushes, conifers, fern and fruit trees.

There are wind chimes in the courtyard area which come to life on breezy days and the owners brighten the area with fairy lights under the pergola. Seriously, you'd think it was Christmas every time they're out there at night.

I reckon I'm lucky to have this wonderful stretch of green and cosiness in the middle of suburbia which I can show off to my friends.

I know Mrs Fixit is loving the space – she's out here often, always humming, and trimming this, cutting that, digging here, spading there, just beautifying the space, which is already as pretty as any portrait of a fancy garden.

I reckon all that's left to do is work out how we can get rid of the lazy, old bugger she married.

# Sentimental Journey

Victor Ferreira was excited. He'd decided he would go on another journey today. He loved that he could still do this. Nothing would ever stop him from doing this, he'd decided. Today was when he'd go back to the country he'd left all those years ago – and connect to the voices, to the sounds of the wonderful people he'd left behind.

Victor recalled the time he'd decided to take his family and leave Africa, just as his parents had left their Mediterranean haven to move to Africa many years before. That was a big decision for Victor – but those were volatile times in Africa. He knew that the best chance for his family's future lay in migration, just as it had been for his parents.

'Are you ready to do this?' Victor had asked Lilian, his wife of ten years.

'Whatever is best for our children,' Lilian had replied.

'Your mother, your father? You'll miss them,' Victor had said.

'Whatever is best for our children,' Lilian echoed her earlier reply.

'Your sister and her daughters?' Victor had asked again.

'Whatever is best for our children.'

To them, it was an upheaval as immense as Mt Kilimanjaro, Africa's highest mountain, leaving their secure jobs, their first home, their families, their friends. But it was the voices, the sounds of the family gatherings that Victor would miss the most…

*

That was then. Today, Victor would be taking the journey, the sentimental journey – and it wasn't long before he was there…

*

Victor was, at last, with his large family. It was a family loud, gregarious and just fun to be with. He was in his element as he arrived at the gathering…kissing everyone on both cheeks as was the tradition. They were all there celebrating the christening of yet another addition to the clan. It was always like this. All their get-togethers were like this.

''Ello, Victor, how are you, my boy?' said a favourite aunt.

'You so big, you must come see your aunty more,' said another.

'Lookit your cheeks, so chubby, Victor. Your wife, she feeds you too well,' said one more, pinching both sides of his boyish face with fingers as wrinkled as the faces of most of his elderly relatives.

'You were a lovely altar boy, Victor, such a good boy,' added yet another aunt.

They spoke as one – as did everyone else in the party. Voices, scores of voices, yet Victor could, with great clarity, hear all of them individually, then together; loud, louder, as they all strived to make themselves heard.

Victor moved over to the men's side. There was always that demarcation. Women on one side, men on the other. It was not sexist, he recalled one of his uncles saying.

'Just tradition, just the way it always has been,' his uncle had said.

The tradition continued at this get-together.

''Ello, Victor, you put on weight, man,' said a favourite uncle.

'Your wife feeding you too much, no?' queried another.

'Fat belly, boy, you pregnant too, then?' said one more uncle, drawing laughter and slaps on his back from those around him.

'When's it due, son?' questioned yet another, patting Victor's belly as it tried to contract into a T-shirt, jammed as tightly as a sardine in a can.

They, too, all spoke over each other. Again, Victor could hear all the voices, but their individual tones were distinct too.

Victor closed his eyes. Sound overwhelmed all other senses. He savoured the commotion, kept it close, clasped it to his chest.

Too soon it was time to go. Victor collected his wife and family, kissed his aunts and uncles, his nephews and nieces, and all the other extended family, and found himself at the car…without his keys.

He knew he had to go back. He also knew what that meant. Once again, he kissed all his aunts and uncles, nephews and nieces, the other extended families, collected the keys, and repeated the kissing again, as he said his second farewell.

Finally, at the car, Victor looked up at his wife.

Lilian was smiling. But her eyes shed tears. He knew she was weeping because they would be leaving all of this behind, this camaraderie, these friendships, companionships, these noises, sounds…

*

Victor Ferreira had been excited because he'd decided earlier in the day to go on another journey. He loved that he could still do this. Nothing would ever stop him from doing this, he'd decided long ago. Today was when he'd gone back to the country he'd left all those years ago – and again connected with the wonderful people he'd left behind.

Victor was ninety. He was also bedridden. He believed, however, that he was a lucky man. He could relive, time and again, his journeys, the journeys of nostalgia, time and time again.

His body had betrayed him but, as yet, his mind had not. While his brain cells still kicked and yelled, he looked forward to making many more sentimental journeys to the voices, to the sounds of his aunts, uncles, nieces and nephews, and their extended families, at those memorable family gatherings, for however much time he had left.

# Body in the Garden

'It's one of the Beaumont children,' Esme Parker from down the road was telling her best friend, Tilly.

'You sure?' Tilly replied. 'Whenever they find a body, it's always one of those poor children.'

'I'm positive,' said Esme. One of the cops told me. He said it's one of them kids that's been missing for yonks – so it has to be.'

Esme, small and stocky, was a pain. Befitting her character, she had a snout which overwhelmed her face so it never surprised anyone she'd ended up with the nickname, Nosey. She'd also never married, so Nosey Parker was the moniker that had stuck for life.

Another thing you could always be assured of with Esme: she was never right. So, one of the Beaumont children it was unlikely to be, but there was a body, so who could it be? Esme, as was her wont, was determined to find out.

Though most of the locals steered clear whenever she came into sight, Esme did have one other person she considered a friend besides Tilly. That mate was Bobby Nutter – the same scruffy, bearded Bobby, nicknamed Nutty, who had no family, friends or acquaintances, except perhaps for Esme.

It was to the pub and Nutty that Esme rushed so she could break the news of the body in the garden. She was confident Nutty would be in the pub, because that's usually where he was. Nutty would find an occasional job in the farming village in which they all lived. He was a damn good worker when he was sober which, sadly, was seldom.

There was a good chance, therefore, that Esme would find Nutty in his favourite watering hole. Of course, Esme dragged Tilly with her.

She wouldn't dream of entering a tavern alone. What would the towns-folk say if they saw her doing that?

'Heard the news?' Esme shouted to Nutty, whom she spotted sitting on his favourite stool in a dark corner of the bar.

Nutty didn't look too pleased to see her. His latest job, cleaning toilets at the council block on the beach, had lasted just two days. He'd found a half-carton of Moselle behind one of the dunnies – and couldn't resist. He was found by the council supervisor curled around a loo at closing-up time. He was fired on the spot.

'What news?' Nutty asked, rolling his eyes.

'Cops found a body in the reserve, behind the rose garden.'

'And?' He knew she couldn't wait to tell him.

'I reckon it's one of the Beaumont kids.'

'Heard that one before.'

'Cop told me. Beefy.'

'Beefy?' Nutty searched the depths of his beer for a memory prod.

'Constable Jackson. That's his nickname. Don't you know any-thing?'

No sooner had Esme relayed the shocking news than the constable himself walked in on the trio.

'This belong to you, Nutty?' the tall, heavily built constable asked, holding up a stained and torn shirt.

'What if it does?' Nutty was accustomed to being harassed by the law.

'Found it near a body at the bottom of the rose garden this morn-ing,' replied the constable. 'It has the initials BN on the collar, so thought it could be yours.'

In a quick, quivering movement, Esme gripped Tilly's arm. Her other hand rose just as swiftly to her mouth to prevent her from scream-ing aloud. It was to no avail. 'Oh my gawd, Nutty,' she howled. 'Was it you?'

'Stop squawking, you silly woman,' Nutty yelled back. 'It's got no-thing to do with me!'

Esme ignored this response. Guilty until proven innocent was always the path to tread for Esme when there happened to be a terrible tale to titillate the townsfolk. 'You're a murderer, Nutty!' she accused. 'Oh, my gawd, Tilly, all this time we've been mixing with a murderer.'

Now it was Constable Jackson's turn to have a go at the hysterical Esme. 'What are you on about, you dizzy woman?' he asked.

'You told me this morning you'd found the kid who'd been missing for yonks – and now you've got the evidence: Nutty's shirt found near the child's body in the garden…' said Esme. She was so elated with her summary her words barely separated from each other as she spluttered them out.

Constable Jackson's attention had diverted from the laid-back Nutty, who'd taken another sip of his ale, utterly confident of his innocence. The policeman instead towered over the short, stocky woman with the long nose. Though years younger than Esme, he seemed as angry as a father about to scold a disrespectful daughter.

'It's people like you who spread nasty rumours about our little town,' the constable bellowed at her. 'It's time you got a life, Esme Parker. Yes, we did find a body. Yes, it happened a while ago. But it wasn't a child. It was a young billy goat – and it died of natural causes.'

# Just Friends

Vivacious Stella Rathbone knew she'd finally made it. It had taken years of hard work and dedication but now she was where she always wanted to be – a successful real estate managerial consultant.

'I should be happy but, damn it, I'm not,' she wondered aloud.

She pondered further on her discontent. 'Is it because of what I've done to get here? The number of people I've hurt?'

She expected to feel pangs of guilt, but ultimately decided she didn't care how many people she'd had to climb over to get to the top. Or climb on top of. Stella wasn't proud of some of her exploits. She knew, however, that she had done what was needed to make her quest for a life of comfort just that bit easier. And, somehow, she'd always managed to keep her flings discreet.

She particularly hoped no one would ever find out about Mr Brown, the company's senior accountant, even though he was married to that terrible woman who did not deserve him.

Those who thought there might have been something between her and Mr Brown were wrong, always had been…except for that one time when they yielded to temptation brought on by the free alcohol dished out at the Christmas party.

It had been a one-off – and had happened many years ago. Mr Brown was already well established within the company and Stella was in the early stage of her scramble up the corporate ladder.

After that night, when they surrendered to their desires in the broom closet under the office stairs, neither ever went to a celebratory office function again. They'd remained friends and never murmured a word about their indiscretion to any other person in the years following.

Neither did they themselves ever mention it. It had been a mistake not to be repeated – and they would never revisit it. It became, for both, an unspoken pact.

There were, of course, some people who suspected they were having an affair, no matter how unsullied the pair believed their relationship.

However, for Stella and Mr Brown, a listening ear was all they expected of each other. Their relationship had always (except, of course, for that one time) been companionable – one born from loneliness – and they'd managed very well to keep it that way.

*

It was with surprise then that in the café near the office where they met once a week for a pre-work coffee, Mr Brown, he of the unruly, brown-as-bark hair, looked at her with his dark brown eyes, and broke the sudden news.

'I want to leave my wife,' Mr Brown said. 'I want to be with you.'

There was a lengthy pause, much longer than the curly, blonde hair which rested lazily on Stella's thin shoulders.

'Why?' she asked eventually. 'I thought we were friends, that we just wanted to be friends.'

'Yes, friends, but I think we need to be friends with accompanying benefits…'

This man she'd valued for so many years as a colleague, companion, confidant now wanted something different from their relationship, something she wasn't sure she wanted.

'No, no…' she said after a while. 'I can't do it.' Stella got up off her chair and left the coffee shop hurriedly, as if she had something urgent to attend to.

In this case, there was.

*

Two days later, having locked herself in her luxuriously furnished double unit, she'd come to the conclusion she hadn't meant what she'd said before fleeing the café.

In her heart, she knew, too, she wanted Mr Brown. He was suave, smart, scrumptious. He always had been. There was no denying it. How had they managed to have a platonic relationship for all these years? Especially after hastily sampling the forbidden fruit that evening of the drunken Christmas party.

It was why, Stella finally concluded, she was unhappy. Materially, she had everything she wanted and needed. Mr Brown was her missing link. Finally, he'd told her it was she whom he wanted, not his detestable wife. How had they been married for fifteen years, she wondered? How had he put up with her? Mrs Brown was selfish, uncouth and unkempt – and had never worked, ever, living instead off the rewards of her husband's long hours of labour.

Mr Brown had only married that woman because he thought she was pregnant, Stella had heard. And she hadn't been with child. Only told him that she was – and later, after they'd hurriedly married, that she'd miscarried. She was a cheat and a liar. Of that, Stella was convinced. Mrs Brown did not deserve her delectable husband.

But Stella knew Mrs Brown would not let her husband go. And, that's why, for the first time in her life, the hard-working, dedicated and disciplined Stella Rathbone's thoughts turned to murder.

# Two of a Kind

Angel never lived up to his name. He was lovable, yes. But disciplined? Organised? Responsible? Reliable? Never. To be fair, those adjectives wouldn't apply to most youngsters but Angel's reputation had, from an early age, become entrenched as the hyperactive, sports-mad kid who unwittingly found himself the butt of jokes.

That had started when he was in primary school, when he was just eight. In particular, that time when he came out of the bathroom with toilet paper dangling from the waist of his oversized jeans.

Angel had always stood out in a crowd. He had a mane of blond, curly locks which he hated to have cut; eyes as blue as the soccer ball he loved to kick around and go to bed with; a smile the size of a bright quarter moon; and cheeks as chubby as the dumplings his mum loved to cook for him.

Angel never noticed the loo paper dangling from his waist that day. That was because it was behind him. In any case, he was in too much of a hurry to get on to the playground to kick around his beloved blue ball.

Everyone else at the school, however, seemed to notice. And no one was telling him of his plight, not even his mates.

Even if they'd had a change of heart, Angel, once on the field, was not stationary long enough to be told he had five pieces of two-ply flowing freely behind him. In full flight, the reams bounced in unison with his golden locks.

Would make a great advert on telly, pondered one of Angel's young aides, Miss Wally, who happened to be on playground duty that day. However, Miss Wally was also somewhat irked. Somebody would have to let the boy know. I guess it'll have to be me, she decided, resolving to run after the little boy to break the news to him.

Meanwhile, Angel, ball on a string as he zigzagged along the field, was a picture of concentration and still oblivious to the item he'd failed to properly dispense of after his pit stop.

Nor did he pay heed to the yells of schoolmates, suddenly raucous with their comments.

'You're disgusting,' shouted one boy.

'That's sick,' giggled a girl loudly.

'Angel's a poo boy,' heckled one unkindly soul.

When Miss Wally heard one young lad (he obviously came from that horrid neighbourhood out of town, she thought) shout out, 'Angel, you sucker, you wiped it – but you didn't get rid of it,' she knew it was time to act.

Off Miss Wally went, discarding the high heels she'd pondered over so carefully before setting off for school that day. Though she had a be-lated inkling it might have been against school rules, she found herself diving through the air and crash-tackling Angel at the precise moment he appeared to have run past her.

'What the…' shouted the astonished boy, as he lay on the ground, his ball no longer dangling from his left boot. Instead, his boot was up the rather flabby backside of Miss Wally, who cut an ungainly figure as she too lay sprawled.

In the seconds it had taken for Miss Wally's tackle to fell Angel, the entire school inexplicably seemed to have formed a circle around the grounded pair.

From nowhere, someone clapped, then disrespectfully shouted once, twice, three times, 'Too young for you, Wally. Too old for you, Angel.'

Others joined in the chant, which became so guttural that, event-ually, the principal, Mrs Sterne, cut a swath through the mass of bodies, and demanded in her booming voice, 'Quiet! Everyone disperse! You, Angel, to my office! And you, too, Miss Wally!'

Many years later, Angel, now grown up, had also grown out of love for soccer. He had become disciplined, organised, responsible, reliable. He'd also fallen for and married a woman, fortunately with a sense of humour. They'd produced one child, a clone of Angel, so much like him, even from birth, that they'd agreed to name him Raphael.

As he got older, the more Raphael resembled his father.

Angel had never left the district and despite the shellacking he'd received in the episode with Miss Wally all those years ago, he was delighted he'd eventually graduated from the campus's high school and that his son was now attending the same primary school.

And tonight was concert night. Of course, Raphael was excited to be cast as one of the elves in the school play; so excited that, minutes before the curtain went up, he just had to spend a penny. Raphael's teacher, too busy to pay him attention, allowed him to go there unattended.

As his parents sat proudly in the audience, Raphael eventually took to the stage. It did not, however, take long before Angel's smile turned to dismay. Stung by a tremor of flashbacks, he watched his young son take up his position…accompanied by numerous strips of Kleenex dangling from the back of his costume.

# Destination Danger

Only very fortunate ones are allowed to get close to this destination for a hurried look, and then leave of their own accord. Most times, you are lured to visit – and never return from where you came.

However, it was time for the four strangers – Phoebe, Matius, Basil and Bethanie – to take their chance and venture into that unfamiliar world, into the destination labelled Danger.

*

For Phoebe, it was a no-brainer. She was bored as a bloated flea by her daily routine. She pandered to her betrothed and to her many brothers and sisters. Goodness knows why, because they treated her badly.

'Food,' demanded Igor, her partner, at the end of every day, even though he seldom did a decent day's work.

'Where's the dessert?' demanded her selfish siblings, even before they'd finished their main meal, over which Phoebe had laboured for hours.

Phoebe wanted something different. She wanted more from life. She was ideally placed to be lured.

Matius was another questioning his life before deciding to venture to the special destination. Matius was tired of being attracted by the bright lights. He knew he was addicted to them, so uninhibitedly that he often put his life in danger. He knew, too, there would be much more trouble beyond these lights. However, he wanted something different and was prepared to take that next step. This new destination fascinated him as much as a little one is captivated by fairy floss.

Phoebe and Matius favoured the indoors, not usually venturing from their regular haunts. Probably also because of the predictability of this environment, they felt it was the right time to shift their zones of comfort, towards this special destination.

Both were in the headspace to be seduced.

*

Outside, meanwhile, Basil continued to have a field day with all the delicacies available to him. He enjoyed the variety, the tasty titbits, but something else attracted him, this very special something that lurked, seemingly always just above his line of sight. It was the forbidden destination, the place he knew would invite trouble if he decided to give it a go. However, he was desperate to reach this place of special interest. He knew, one day, he would just do it.

Joining Basil outside in eyeing this special site was Bethanie.

She flitted about her vast arena, showing off her wares. She knew she looked beautiful, dressed never-endingly and so splendidly in almost all colours of a rainbow. Neither was she afraid to parade her stunning curves.

Many were envious of her. Bethanie knew that. She didn't care. She was alive, free-spirited, and majestically magnificent.

Bethanie was also exceedingly curious and desired desperately to enter the special place where most feared to tread, yet were dying to do so.

*

The day finally came when all four decided to throw caution to the breeze. They would farewell their families, knowing they were taking a big gamble, but not wishing to tell them what they were about to do for fear of being dissuaded from their goal.

Their target of reaching that destination – always so near, so mysterious, so tempting – was in sight, and they did not wish to be deterred from attaining it. It was a place where they believed they would be welcomed with shameless affection, with glee, with tight hugs and squeezes, but which they also knew could be the place from which there might be no coming back.

In fact, there were two destinations.

The inside one, dubbed Pleasure Palace by those in the know, coaxed Phoebe and Matius. The outside one, called the Blissful Bastion, attracted Basil and Bethanie.

So it came to pass when all four hastened into peril.

As they took their inevitable flights into danger, insiders Phoebe the fly and Matius the moth, and outsiders Basil the beetle and Bethanie the butterfly wavered for mere seconds.

Even so, it was too late.

All four succumbed, all on the same day, all quite separately and coincidentally.

As a well-fitting glove rapidly envelops fingers, so were they swiftly ensnared by those most delicate of dangerous traps, those sinister of sultry destinations, those places of no return – the spiders' webs.

# Too Close to Call

She lay on a lush lawn among dry, fallen leaves…and wished she were anywhere except here, here where she had to help her child make a very important decision.

Nadia Nijinski's life, at forty, was again in turmoil, even though she'd just won a lucrative position as head chef at one of Australia's five-star hotels.

*

A woman of many talents, Nadia had, long before she left school, harboured a desire to become a model. With high cheekbones, mesmerising grey eyes and the presence of a mystic, Nadia made the most of her parents' Asian features. Hong Kong residents, they'd fled that country in the 1960s as boat people.

Nadia recalled the many auditions she'd undergone on her catwalk quest. Sadly, she was considered by agencies to be too tiny to be a model. A mere five 'and a bit' feet meant she'd often be dwarfed by other women on the ramp, despite diligently training herself to don six-inch stilettos to overcome her vertical deficiency.

'You're gorgeous, but you don't have it,' one agent told Nadia.

'Have what?' she asked.

'A key ingredient,' he replied.

'What's missing?' she asked.

'You're a midget,' he responded.

Her modelling career had ended suddenly, brutally.

Nadia, however, was never born to be a shrinking violet. Usually feisty and self-assured, she decided on an alternative route to fame and prosperity. She was destined to become a fashion designer, she decided, specifically a designer of small but spectacular hats. She often wore her own fascinators, intricately designed and admired by many A-listers.

'You need to start your own business,' said her father.

'Your hats are exceptional,' said her mother.

She toyed with the idea for some months, gratified by her parents' support of the magic she could produce with head pieces, feathers, flowers and beads.

But fate was to play her a hand as heartlessly as the agent who'd mocked her in her stab at catwalk fame.

At eighteen, Nadia fell pregnant after a one-night stand. It was the culmination of a liaison which threatened to disgrace her family's name among the Hong Kong expats living in the wealthy enclave in Sydney.

'You must get rid of the child,' said her father.

'It will destroy your life – and ours – if you have it,' said her mother.

Without her parents' support, as well as that of the coward who left the country soon after Nadia had told him of her plight, she had no option but to abort the foetus.

Her resourcefulness shattered, Nadia gave up on her fashion idea – illogically linking it with her plight. She was too ambitious, she'd decided.

With regular meditation and yoga, Nadia worked hard at rebuilding her confidence. She also diligently learned to cook in her parents' Asian restaurant in her quest to get her life on an even keel.

However, the trauma of deliberately losing a child continued to weigh heavily. An arranged marriage, which did not last, but which led to the birth of a daughter, Angelica, by the time she was twenty-three, helped lift Nadia's gloom.

She renewed her quest to reach for the stars. She became renowned for her extraordinary cooking skills which made her parents' restaurant one of the most sought-after in the state.

A prearranged visit by a prominent five-star hotel owner to the family's restaurant eventually led to an offer to work at his hotel.

'What's in it for me?' she asked the man.

'Lifetime security in terms of finance – as well as accommodation.'

'What about Angelica, my daughter?' asked Nadia.

'She will be well looked after at all times.'

With the support of her proud parents, Nadia accepted the job.

Now, two months after being appointed, she believed her life's path finally had been settled.

But fate had not had its fill of toying with Nadia Nijinski's life.

*

Angelica, Nadia's seventeen-year-old daughter, approached her just days after finishing high school. Beautiful and especially smart, Angelica was about to set out on a career in medicine, a path she had chosen and one wholeheartedly supported by her mother and grandparents.

This particular morning, though, having wrestled through a torturous night, Angelica was in tears.

'What's wrong, darling?' Nadia asked.

Her daughter's hands encircled her mother's waist as tightly as a child holds on to a parent's hand in a busy train terminal. There were no words; just an odd sobbing sound emanated from Angelica's mouth.

'Angelica, what's the matter, darling?'

'Mum…'

'Angelica, what is it?'

'Mum, I'm pregnant…'

*

Nadia lay on the hotel's lush lawn among the dry, fallen leaves…and wished she were anywhere except here, here where she had to help her daughter make a decision which would affect the rest of her life.

# No Place to Go

She was frantic with anxiety. News of the bushfire had spread through the community. How was she to cope? How was she going to manage if the fire in the bush came her way? Her husband had gone walkabout with the mob. He'd left days ago. He would be far away. Isolated. He would have no idea of the danger facing his family.

Word was that the fire would reach their abode within hours. What if it arrived sooner? she thought. What if I can't get all my family together in the time I have? They were spread far and wide. The children had decided to go off on their own, become more independent. They were old enough to do so. She had not been happy about their decision. But they had to live their lives too. They needed space for their families too.

Only one little one remained at home to be cared for. She thought she could cope with that responsibility. What she could not cope with was the sight, the smell, the sound, the heat…of bushfire.

*

She recalled the time before when they'd barely escaped its clutches.

She remembered the sight of it. Red. Glowing red. Like the sun, just before dusk. Except it wasn't a pleasant spectacle. The sun going down at dusk was magical. The bushfire red she recalled was anything but. She imagined the fire of hell, the red flames licking at you, slowly at first, then engulfing you. The bushfire red would be like those flames.

She could still smell the smoke, the smoke that made it so difficult to breathe, the smoke that suffocated. There had been nothing else they could do, except move hurriedly away from the area from where the smoke came.

She remembered especially the sound of that bushfire. Some compared it to the sound of a jet engine before take-off. She wouldn't know. She'd never been near a plane. The sound of a rampant bushfire was also like the sound of a speeding freight train, it was thought. She wouldn't know. She'd never been near a train. She wouldn't know because she was a homebody. She didn't like to leave home. Not like her husband. Not like her older children.

The sound of that fire, the one before – to her, it was like the roar of rumbling thunder. She'd heard lots of thunder in her life. The sound of thunder in the bush was like echoes of alien noise colliding. No gaps. Just rumbling roars of continuous thunder. She'd wondered at that time if that sound would ever stop.

The heat, as the fire got closer, became unbearable. She'd heard that the intense heat killed you. Not the flames of the fire themselves. She realised why. She imagined it was like being a grub on a wood fire, a grub dying from the heat, before the flames got it.

To this day, she could not believe she hadn't died, that her family had not perished. There had been a wind change, it was said. At the death. As the heat became more intense, as the balls of flames prepared to grasp, to envelop her and her family, it decided, God decided, it was not her time. It was not her family's time.

She'd already got to the point of shutting her eyes, expecting to feel the intense heat, then, most likely, the burning, the burning, the burning…

*

Pull yourself together, she told herself. She wasn't sure how long she'd been thinking about the last time. It was silly doing that. It was silly to be thinking of the last time, she again told herself, especially as she did not have her family together.

She realised again there was nothing she could do this time. She was alone. The lone adult. With the little one.

Time passed as listlessly as it must for those on death row.

It wasn't long, though, before she heard all the familiar sounds of the bushfire, the new bushfire. Twigs, branches, trees…snapping, cracking. Snapping, cracking. She looked up. Fireballs leaped across the tops of trees, which exploded before her eyes. Smoke smells were already suffocating.

Not again, she whispered.

Not again.

Please, not again.

She was not going to be lucky this time, she thought. She'd had her blessed escape. She and her family had had their miracle. This time, there would be no mercy.

Frantic with anxiety, she could no longer bear to look at the fireballs as they moved hastily in on her.

On her, and her little one.

She closed her eyes tightly, shielding, as best as she could, the joey in her pouch.

# Her Pick

Freddie Murphy looked fondly at Christine through bloodshot eyes. He wasn't weary after a big night out. Rather, it had been another big day at work. It wasn't the best of jobs, cleaning railway station loos. It wasn't something he looked forward to any day. The graffiti – often porn, seldom humorous – scrawled on puke-brown walls or the stinking leftovers of strangers dashing from urgent pit stops were never pleasant. But it was a job. And Freddie was doing his best. He was never given the chance to become educated so he could do something better.

At least, however, he was the one who'd decided to smash the mould. While the rest of his family were a bunch of deadbeats, he'd chosen another way, a different path. He'd been in the job for nearly eighteen  months. His relatives ridiculed him, but he let their criticism wash over him.

Freddie stretched out muscular, tatt-covered biceps, and welcomed Christine into a tight embrace. Now it was up to her, his girlfriend. She had a choice to make.

*

Christine and her mother, Eileen, stared at each other across the room, neither wishing to be first to look away.

They resembled a matching set – greasy, blonde hair cut into bobs, that tinge of sunflower in velvet eyes, and tiny, straight noses nestled in the midst of high cheekbones. Eileen's worry lines were the only giveaway to one of a more advanced age.

Most times, the pair got on. This wasn't to be one of those times.

After setting up the potential skirmish, Eileen fired the first salvo.

She got to the point in a hurry. 'Christine, you've not got this right, love.'

No retaliation.

So Eileen continued, 'Use your looks and brains to your advantage – don't waste them on a no-hoper.'

Christine bit her bottom lip with front teeth in desperate need of a makeover. The jagged edges detracted from her appearance – and always made her feel insecure. There was still no verbal response, but her lip chewing and habit of twirling both her ear lobes were giveaway signs of anxiety.

Eileen treated the stillness as a go-ahead for another shot. 'I'm heart-broken that my only child is defying me. After all I've done for you. Why'd you want to be associated with a family like the Murphys?'

Her daughter appeared muzzled so Eileen pulled the trigger. 'You'll regret it one day, my girl. Take it from one who knows.'

At last, Christine charged into battle. 'What the hell would you know?' she spat. 'You know zilch, nothing, nada about anything – least of all love.'

Eileen had anticipated anger. Still, she was taken aback by the venom of her daughter, the child who'd always done as she was told. 'How can you say that about me?' said Eileen. 'I left your father to pro-tect us, to protect you, from his violence. I loved him…but I loved you more.'

'You've never cared about me,' screamed Christine. 'You only care about hobnobbing with those suck-holes at work.'

Eileen felt tears tickle her eyelids at the offensive assessment of her supportive work-mates. She decided to get back to the point. 'You might be naive, but you're not stupid,' said Eileen. 'You've seen the people who go to our supermarket and the way they live. You're only seventeen – you're too young to know your own mind.'

'I might be seventeen, but I know what I want – bitch!'

Eileen recoiled. Her daughter had never spoken to her this way. She'd brought her up to be polite, well-mannered. Frantic, she decided not to retreat. 'The estate's a dump for no-hopers,' she said. 'The Murphy family, including Freddie, are scumbags. That is no life for you.' Desperate, she commanded, 'I don't want you to see him again!'

If Eileen saw the flash of flesh heading towards her, she was as slow to move as any Centrelink queue. The blow from her daughter hit her like that first shock of the drill at a dentist. But it wasn't the blow, stinging as it was, that wounded her. It was the act itself, the slap across her face, a strike which brought back so many terrifying memories of a violent marriage.

*

Christine had to make a choice, a choice which could be for life.

Would it be her mother? The woman who'd left her husband because he beat her up? The woman who'd sacrificed so much of her life to bring Christine up in a safe and caring environment? The woman she'd just slapped?

Or would it be Freddie, the boy with the tatts, with the lavatory-cleaning job, the boy whose family had, for generations, sucked dry the dole? The boy who'd chosen to shatter the mould?

It was a choice Christine had decided to make.

# The Chosen One

'Pick me, pick me!' Pine Nut whispered as he watched two young children and their father walk along the rows and rows of similar shapes and sizes.

He didn't think he'd stand a chance of being selected. All the others seemed more mature, more defined, more shapely. But they were heading straight towards him. He was fretful, yet buoyant. Would he be the Chosen One? Just like his Mum and Nanna before him…

*

Pine Nut had grown from a littlie into a likely lad with the perfectly formed body, as curvy as any of the pretenders before him.

He recalled the stories of Prickly Patty (his mum) and Messy Tessy (his nanna) about the joys and disappointments of being the Chosen One, the centre of attention, at festive time.

They had told him that adults loved the smell of them. Prickly Patty, Messy Tessy and their many friends' distinct scent pervaded whichever house they were assigned to, no matter how large or cosy.

For the children, it was the glitter, the ornaments, the tinsel and the bright lights which adorned their centre of attention. All of this made them love this time of the year…not to mention the many gifts placed neatly underneath large boughs.

Pine Nut's mum had told him what she'd loved most about the morning after Christmas Eve. 'The *ooohs* and *aaahs* from the children,' Prickly Patty had said. She'd enjoyed, too, listening to the screeches of delight as the youngsters diligently, at first, then later feverishly tore at the colourful wrappings hiding gifts brought to them by the jolly man on the children's day of all days. 'I'd feel as if I was a part of the family, the part that made the family so content on that very special day of the year,' he'd remembered Prickly Patty telling him. 'Even though I'd been an early arrival, I'd always felt as welcome as the cheery fellow in his red suit,' she'd added.

There were also things which did not please Pine Nut's many relatives and extended family. Being cut to size was very painful, he'd recalled hearing.

'It was sudden, but still a shock,' a family friend had said.

Neither was it enjoyable to be sandwiched between heavy, jagged rocks in a large crate to prevent a catastrophic collapse on the big day.

'The heavy decorations weighed me down terribly,' was another lament.

'Whoever decided to plonk a solid star right on top of my head – well, that person should have to play Pick-Up-Stix with needles as punishment,' was one more response.

Pine Nut heard more things his older relatives were disgruntled about at what was meant to be the happiest time of the year.

'I never got a drink,' one had said, adding: 'You can't count the family dog peeing down my bottom. I used to shudder whenever it lifted its leg – they didn't know, because Growler usually did it out of sight of the rest of the family.'

Another gripe was the hundreds of little lights that were constantly left on and often flickered all night long, for many, many evenings… this never made for a decent night's sleep.

Finally, the most unpleasant experience was when families decided that their visitors – even well-behaved, nice-smelling ones – were no longer welcome.

Pine Nut recalled seeing Prickly Patty and Messy Tessy being taken back to the tree lot – and dumped. And, later, he'd watched, with sadness, as they were shovelled away, transformed into bits of bark, then left to lie in all sorts of weather around other trees or plants in many strangers' gardens.

The family of three at the tree lot approached Pine Nut. By this time, his reminiscing about his Mum, Nanna and other relatives had led to second thoughts.

There seemed to be a lot more cons than pros to this deal. Perhaps he did not want to be the Chosen One this year – or any other year for that matter.

As he continued to weigh up the positives and negatives of being the Christmas season's centre of attention, he saw the father of the two children point directly at him and say, 'Here's a stud – he'll be just right beside the fireplace in the lounge, out of the snow, warming the cockles of our hearts…yes, he's the one.'

Pine Nut flushed with self-importance. He almost turned a lighter shade of red, though he knew that might be stretching his embarrassment. Fancy being called a stud, he thought. And having the ability to warm the cockles of a young family's heart… Prickly Patty and Messy Tessy would have been so proud of him.

Seconds later, Pine Nut heard the screeching sound of an electric saw. His fate, whether he liked it or not, had been sealed.

# Moment in Time

Samantha Radcliffe found a corner in the room. She surveyed the scene. It was chaotic. She recognised the faces of friends and relatives amid the commotion. The noise was overwhelming.

Background music had long ago faded into a non-existent vacuum as drinks clinked and people acknowledged each other, chattering in the same shattering way clusters of corellas communicate in cosy country quarters.

In spite of herself, Samantha smiled at the bedlam. She had greeted all of her guests with that smile. It was her trademark. When she smiled, the dimples seemed to dive through her chubby cheeks so deep were the indents.

Throughout this special day, however – her eighteenth birthday – she'd felt uneasy. Something was not quite right. She'd tried to dismiss it. It was a big occasion and eighty people were in attendance. She had every right to feel anxious.

But one person was missing. To her, he was the most important individual of all. And his absence made her worry. It was already eight p.m. and he still hadn't arrived.

'Heard from Zac?' Samantha's Mum cosied into the corner with her daughter.

'No, Mum.'

'Hmm. He couldn't reach you for some reason so he rang earlier to tell me he had to pick up his suit at the dry cleaners – and he'd be here soon after.'

'I'm starting to worry, Mum.'

'No message, honey?'

'No, Mum, nothing.'

'Probably got caught up on the beach. Knowing him, even today he'd go for a quick surf before picking up the suit.'

'I guess.' This time, Samantha's smile left no indents on her face.

Her mobile rang. Samantha did not recognise the number. The smart phone indicated it was from someone not listed on her database. She was tempted to let it ring out. At the last minute, she took the call.

She stepped out of the noisy room.

*

Zac Radcliffe was running late. He knew he shouldn't have gone down to the beach, especially today. Especially tonight. It was going to be a big occasion and he didn't want to let anyone down. Especially Samantha. He knew he meant the world to her and he didn't want to disappoint her.

But the lure of the surf was irresistible. It called, and he had to go. It was like a drug. It was there and he had to have it, no matter what. Even if it got him in trouble.

'Perfect waves,' he purred as he slid into his wetsuit. He'd pick up the other suit, the dress suit, for tonight's big party on the way to Samantha's, he decided.

Time was of no consequence when Zac was out at sea. One sound continuously filled his senses – the echo of waves crashing, again and again and again. Enveloped in this idyllic world, Zac always lost a sense of time. This occasion was no different.

Only when he got back to shore did Zac realise he wasn't going to be punctual. He'd have to move – as quickly as he could. Even then, he knew he would be late. And, in trouble, especially with his mum and Samantha.

*

'Hello, who's this?' Samantha asked into the phone after she had stepped out of the noisy room.

'Congratulations, Samantha – you've turned eighteen at last!'

'Who is this?' she asked again, not recognising the distinctive tones.

'My name's Indira. I'm phoning on behalf of Bupa. Now that you're eighteen, you know it's never too early to start an insurance plan.'

'How'd you get my name?' Samantha, her nerves as taut as a guitar string, screamed into the phone. Before the caller could reply, she yelled, 'Never mind. Not interested!'

Furious at the invasion of privacy and the timing of the call, Samantha re-entered the room. As she did so, she spotted her mother listening into the mobile she held to her left ear, the index finger of her other hand plunged deeply into her right ear as she struggled to hear above the din.

Suddenly, staring straight at her daughter as if there was no other person in the room, Samantha's mother let out a scream so shrill it stopped all other sounds in the space.

All the chatter, the laughter, the shrieks, even the background music seemed to die at that moment.

It was the instant, too, that Samantha knew her life would never be the same.

Despite not hearing a word from her mother, now sobbing hysterically into the shoulder of her father, Samantha knew Zac would not be coming tonight.

In fact, she knew, without any doubt, her brother, Zac, the boy with the identical dimples to the twin sister he adored, would never be coming home again.

# The Big Decision

The bed shook. It woke me up. Afraid, I wondered where I was. Then I remembered: I'd had to make the Big Decision.

*

It was my fiftieth birthday, the day those of us lucky enough to reach such a milestone had marked with a big red ring on our calendars.

That was the day everyone knew as Decision Day, the day mankind had earmarked as that special one when you decided whether to keep going forward in time or start going back, to become older or younger.

Decision Day was an important one for many millions on Earth, depending on whether or not they were turning fifty.

Depending on my decision, tomorrow – the day after my birthday – I'd be fifty plus one day or fifty minus one day. So, in ten years' time, I'd be sixty – or forty years of age.

Since time immemorial, this was the fate of humans on Earth. On your fiftieth birthday, it was compulsory that your decision to become older or younger be fed into the Analytic Human Processor, stored at the heavily guarded State Control Centre. Different areas of your body were then wired to the processor, a switch flicked and, bingo, your body started to age – or become younger.

It was as simple as that.

The only physical sign the Big Decision had been made was slight burn marks left on the body because of the wiring procedure.

*

Just because it had been this way for eons didn't make my decision easier.

My parents had decided to grow old, and had got older – and sicker, even frail – and their parents before them had chosen to do the same, as had all of my ancestors.

My parents weren't impressed by my decision to even think about going backwards in age.

'You realise that if you live for another fifty years, you'll find yourself in a womb – and that'll be that,' said my papa, nursing a toe stricken by gout.

'Yes, but at least I'll know there's a good chance I'll be around for another fifty years and I can prepare for that,' I told him. 'Nobody in our family has ever hit the century mark, so I'd be the first…well, sort of.'

'What if you get married and have a little one?' shouted my deaf but still astute mama. 'When your child is twenty-five, you'll be the same age. What then?'

'For a start, I'm fifty, remember? That means marriage is unlikely. If it happens and I have a kid, we could hang out together. Play golf, footy…go camping.'

'And when he's forty, you'll be ten,' said Papa, proud of his arithmetic skills.

'Well, we could still hang out. I would've lost my driving licence, so he'd just have to make my lunches, get me dressed and take me to school. That would be cool.'

'My son, I think you need to think very carefully…'

I ignored my papa's pessimism. Excited rather than daunted by the idea of becoming younger, I continued, 'I think what will be even cooler is that all the mistakes I made when I was of a certain age, I wouldn't make again.'

They didn't appear convinced, but I continued, 'Remember, when I mucked around at uni, drinking, partying and gambling, wasting your finances…well, that wouldn't happen this time round. Think of all the money you'd save.'

'Money isn't everything,' said Mama, who knew she was lying.

'And that girl Katrina who I nearly married,' I added, ignoring my mother. 'Remember how you were so close to becoming in-laws? She only turned me down because I wouldn't shave off my beard. Only much later, I realised how stupid I'd been. Well, that wouldn't happen again.'

Papa was shaking his head. 'It seems you've made your decision, my son,' he said. 'It's seldom that people make this choice but you have always been different. We beg of you to have one final think on your own before you go to the Control Centre to make your decision.'

'I will, Papa,' I said, hugging them.

I loved my parents, but this was my decision.

I went to my bedroom, lay on the bed, pondering for the final time which way to go. Grow older or younger? Younger or older? Older or younger?

*

Again, the bed shook. Afraid, I realised that it was mine.

Awake now, I hoped my nightmare about having to make the Big Decision was just that.

Abruptly, though, I was filled with dread.

It wasn't because the bed was still shaking. It was because I looked down at my body and saw slight welts on my chest, arms and legs, welts that weren't there before, welts that looked like faded burn marks.

# Dirty Dog

Henry Black opened the front door to find his best mate curled up in the foetal position. 'Buffy, what's the matter, darlin'?'

The black Labrador didn't move. Instead, she looked at her owner with eyes that first bewildered Henry, then made him very angry. Henry noted, too, the patches of almost-dried blood covering Buffy's jaw and right ear. This hadn't just happened, he knew. She would've been in agony for a while.

Henry bent down, closer to his dog's side, to check for further damage. After a quick inspection, he injected the animal.

Henry had access to a lot of drugs on his property. That's because he ran his business, Henry Black – Greytown Vet, from home.

'Bastards!' he yelled. 'Who would do this to you?'

He covered Buffy with a blanket to reduce the shock and to assist the flow of the injected painkiller.

Henry was used to seeing animals in states so shocking he often wondered why he'd chosen his profession. However, this was something else – this was his beloved Buffy, his loyal friend, the dog he'd spent years of his life with, the one he was as close to as butter on a slice of toast.

'This is a case for Brayden, I reckon,' Henry said.

Brayden Grimes was Greytown's only police officer. If anyone would be keen to track down the scum who'd battered Buffy, it would be the policeman.

Officer Grimes wasn't the most personable human being. Curt to the point of rudeness, he had no time for fools. However, if there was a crime to be solved in his small community, especially those involving animals, he was the man to call on.

Officer Grimes owned his own farm and a liquorice-all-sorts of creatures roamed his vast land.

'Don't you worry, Henry, I'll find this ratbag,' the policeman told the vet at the crime scene. 'And, just between you and me, he'll be roughed up a bit before he finds himself in a lonely police cell.'

Several casual helpers worked on Officer Grimes's farm. It was a workload-heavy property. Being the lone policeman in the town of only five hundred, including neighbouring districts, he didn't have time to do all the work on his own.

One of his helpers was Max Fletcher, a gardener by trade, but also a general maintenance man. When sober, Max, who always wore a grey beanie and matching overcoat, no matter the weather, was a solid worker. However, when he succumbed to the black ales he was overly fond of, Max became a different character.

Just recently, Officer Grimes had caught Max stumble away drunkenly from the chicken coop at the farm.

'What you up to, Max?' Officer Grimes had asked.

'Nuffin' mate, nuffin' to do with ya,' Max had replied, his hands criss-crossed across his chest, as if cradling something.

'You hiding something there, pal?'

'Tole you, I got nuffin'.'

The fact that Max was not wearing his beanie was a telling clue to even a novice policeman that the gardener was, indeed, concealing something. As his foot ricocheted off a large rock along the pathway, Max stumbled and fell, dropping half a dozen eggs which had been cradled in his beanie.

'Nuffin', eh?' Officer Grimes had parodied the gardener, who remained sprawled amid splattered yolks.

Though he'd given Max a warning and a last chance, Officer Grimes was wary of Max after that. He'd surprised himself by keeping Max on. He didn't believe in being soft, even on petty criminals. But, when ale-free, Max was worth his weight in any precious metal. And he'd not put a foot wrong since the stolen eggs incident.

Until the day he noticed Max swaying again. That was just days after the dog bashing. Again, the gardener's headgear was the giveaway.

'What's that on your beanie, mate?' asked Officer Grimes.

'Nuffin',' replied Max.

Officer Grimes's mouth shaped into an inverted half-moon. He'd heard that denial before. 'Nothing? Looks suspiciously like something to me, mate.'

'Tole you there's nuffin' on me beanie.'

'Let's have a closer look then,' said the policeman.

Max wasn't game for face-to-face interaction. With a backward glance, he shot off, quickly followed by the fitter policeman, who had no trouble chasing his victim – and bringing Max down with a tackle that would have earned a best-on-ground award in the local footy comp.

'What's that on your beanie?' Officer Grimes asked again, dusting himself off.

Max didn't have to reply – the beanie was splattered with dried blood.

'You been anywhere near the vet's house, mate?' Officer Grimes asked him.

'What vet? What house?'

'Don't try and con me, mate. Empty your pockets!'

'Tole you I got nuffin'.'

Officer Grimes forced Max to strip off his coat. In a pocket was a haul of drugs, clearly marked, 'Henry Black – Greytown vet'.

Too close to home, Officer Grimes had unearthed the scumbag dog basher.

# Twirl of Fortune

'Ladies and gentlemen,' yelled Ramon, the presenter. 'We have two men and a boy vying for the best of the best. As you know, we have three watches. One is a yellow gold Rolex, worth fifty grand. The others are fakes. Who will be our lucky winner?'

*

The three players had entered the television competition called *Most Deserving*. In less than two hundred words, entrants had to write in, telling a secret panel of three judges why winning the real Rolex could change lives, theirs or others. Thousands had entered – and the two men and a boy were named finalists. Tonight, the winner would take home the big prize.

It would be decided by chance, nothing but sheer good luck.

*

'So, finalist number one, Tom, tell us briefly why you managed to make it this far,' said Ramon.

'I wanted to win so I could donate money to the Red Cross,' said the man.

'That's noble. Why the Red Cross?'

'They help people worldwide, not just in Oz. I think it's a worthy cause.'

'Good idea, Tom – and unselfish, too.'

The audience roared their approval.

'Who's our second competitor?' Ramon prompted.

'I'm Dick.'

'Ahh, the retired pensioner. Why should you win the yellow gold Rolex?'

'My wife hasn't got long to live. She'll be OK for another six months say doctors, and she's always wanted to go on a round the world cruise.'

'Ah-ha,' said Ramon. 'You want to grant her final wish?'

'Yes, fifty grands' worth of Rolex will make for a wonderful month at sea for her.'

'Well, if you win it, looks as if you'll be hitting the high seas too, Dick.'

Boisterous applause reverberated through the room.

'And so, to our last finalist – Harry. How old are you, son?' asked Ramon.

'Just turned seventeen.'

'And what brings you here?'

'I'm smart,' said Harry, grinning. 'But my sister is smarter.'

'Big of you to admit it,' said Ramon. 'So, your sister's clever. So what?'

'She wants to do law at university.'

'So why can't she?'

'My parents have been retrenched. They haven't got enough to cover her years of study.'

'So selling the real-deal Rolex will pay your sister's way?'

'Yes,' agreed Harry.

Again the crowd shrieked their appreciation.

'So, ladies and gentlemen, we have three worthy contenders,' said Ramon. 'Surprise, surprise…Tom, Dick and Harry…who will win the real Rolex?'

'Tommy, Tommy, Tommy,' screamed his supporters.

'Dickie, Dickie, Dickie,' yelled another corner of the room.

'Harry, Harry, Harry,' came a third response.

'So…a bit of quiet please, everyone,' said Ramon. 'This is the big moment, the moment when someone will be a genuine Rolex watch richer. Will it be Tom, the noble Red Cross saviour? Dick, the pensioner who wants to grant his wife her dying wish? Or Harry, the boy who wants to put his smarter sibling through university?'

The audience screamed their favoured name…'Tommmy, Dickkkky, Harrrrry…'

'Now, to win the Rolex worth fifty grand, you all know what will be happening next,' said Ramon. 'We'll spin the bottle once, that's one time only, and whoever it points to, or is closest to…yes, we have the measuring tape, just in case…that person, either one of the two men, or the young lad, will win the yellow gold Rolex watch. The other two competitors will, of course, also win watches, but not the real deal. They will be worth something, of course, but nothing like the yellow gold Rolex worth how much?'

'Fifty grand,' yelled the gathering with the fervour of a bingo mob.

'Now, ladies and gentlemen, I have this bottle. It's a Coke bottle, of course. Because Coke is the major sponsor, with Rolex, of this competition. And I will spin this Coke bottle how many times?'

'Once, once,' yelled the audience, impatient now for an outcome, any outcome.

'Are we all ready?' asked Ramon.

'Yes,' the throng replied, the anxious competitors too.

Ramon moved to the middle of the large table, around which sat the two men and the boy. He held the bottle firmly between his thumb and first two fingers. Ramon had practised this many times. He knew he daren't let it slip from his grasp. It had happened once before in practice. He didn't want it to happen again. Over and over, he'd practised the manoeuvre. He had to get it right – to be fair to the three competitors and, more importantly, not to embarrass himself on national television.

'Here we go!' he said.

It was the perfect spin. The bottle barely budged from the spot he'd placed it. It spun and spun. Round and round. The audience screamed for it to stop. Round and round it went. It's too good a spin, Ramon thought…it's never going to stop. Round and round, it continued to revolve.

Then slowly, ever so slowly, it lost speed. Gently, it appeared to come to rest. Finally, it stopped.

It pointed directly, smack bang, in the middle of one of the three finalists.

'Yaaaayyy, yaaayyy,' he screamed, high-jumping into the night like an Olympic pole vaulter, 'I've won, I've won.'

# Trappings of Success

David Fixit was shattered. The man he'd idolised, looked up to, tried to imitate, was dead – at the age of only forty-seven. David was particularly distraught because that man was his father.

It took David a long time to get over his dad's death. He told his story to friends, acquaintances and even sometimes to strangers while he stood at bus stops waiting to get to or from his dreary job as an operator in a call centre only two kilometres from his home.

He'd relate that his deceased father had smoked a pack and a half daily, had drunk plenty of cheap alcohol – usually at night while stressed about his failing deli business – and enjoyed eggs, bacon and chips, always with sauce, of a morning, every morning, for what was to be his very short life.

After months of sad feelings and wondering whether life was worth living (David was a bachelor, had no siblings nor relatives, and his mum had died of kidney problems some years before), David woke one morning with a plan to turn his life around.

'No,' David said firmly to himself, that morning when the lights went on in his head, 'I'm not going to be a victim like my father.'

He decided to start up a business which would focus on helping people live their lives in a manner different from the way his dad had lived his life.

From the insurance payout he'd eventually received – one thing his father did right was to insure everything he owned – David set out on a path to not only make his life healthy, but those of friends, acquaintances and even strangers.

The name of the business, David believed, would be one of the most important decisions he would make. As well-being was the key, he brainstormed names using HEALTH as an acronym.

Ignoring the extra word in He Eats And Links This To Happiness, David thought that label could work. How Enormous And Lazy The Human was another. Even the rather naughty How Eating And Loving Teaches Happiness and the ugly He Eats And Loves To Heave came to mind as he tried to think, fruitlessly, outside the square.

Finally, David realised the answer lay clearly before him – and his company, Mr Fixit, was born.

David worked diligently over many years to spread his message, the gist of which was that eating the right foods, exercising regularly, sleeping well, and avoiding alcohol and cigarettes would ensure a long life for all, including, of course, his friends, acquaintances and even strangers.

Over two decades, his words of wisdom spread wide and far thanks to the reach of radio, television, newspapers and social media. His name, David Fixit, became synonymous with success. He became the darling of the media, vying for coverage with more established and in-novative entrepreneurs. Dubbed 'The Dashing Bachelor' – there was hardly time for him to sleep let alone build relationships – David, as the years went on, employed more staff, bought more jets, dined with the rich, and had fun with the famous.

Until one morning.

It was just like any other morning, really. David had crawled into bed in the early hours after a midnight meeting, his sixth of the day, at which he'd consumed a large plate of caviar and chilli prawns, washed down with quite a few glasses of his now favourite Moët champagne.

As he lay in his king-sized waterbed, Cuban cigar in hand, wondering about the business from his previous meeting and pondering on the busy day ahead, David thought about his dad who'd died all those years ago.

He'd been so busy, he realised, that it had been a long time since he'd thought about his father. He wondered if his dad would have been proud of Mr Fixit, the company David had built up with little more than a meagre inheritance.

He felt sure his dad would have glowed at the success he had made of his life, just as he knew all of his friends and acquaintances would, too. There were no strangers in his life any longer, thought David, only countless close mates and associates.

He blushed a little at this self-satisfied appraisal.

He also looked forward to yet another hearty breakfast of free-range eggs, top-grade bacon and the crispiest chips, topped with big dollops of the spiciest sauces, at the luxurious Swiss hotel he'd slept in overnight before his next stop in Monaco.

David hopped eagerly out of bed. He stretched his arms to the heavens, allowing his paunch, which had grown to resemble a rather large watermelon, to slip gently down towards his knees – and dropped down dead.

As with his beloved dad, he, too, was just forty-seven.

# Time Out

He stood there, watching, waiting and wondering what he should do next.

He'd had a good day so far. It was lovely being on holidays, particularly on your own, away from the family.

'Look, don't get me wrong,' he'd said earlier, to no one in particular. 'I love my family but they do expect a lot from me. I'm the breadwinner and always will be. I'm expected to do everything, winter or summer. That's fine. I accept that responsibility. But I've had enough – I need a break to rest and recuperate.'

Larry enjoyed life, particularly as he no longer worked full-time. He'd reached an age when it was okay to have holidays on his own.

His wife, the beautiful and understanding Priscilla, didn't mind. She knew it was important for Larry to find a spot on his own to rest his weary bones. He'd done it before and it had done wonders for their relationship. Just thinking of the romance that resurfaced – after he'd returned from some of his time-outs – sent shivers down her delicately sexy spine.

So the pair decided it was time for Larry to catch up with welcoming mates in a neighbouring household, somewhere where he could do what he wanted, by himself, for a while.

Larry opted this time to pop into friends he wasn't quite sure about. He needn't have worried. When they saw him, they were as excited as anyone welcoming seldom-visiting relatives.

'It's Larry,' they cried. 'He's back!'

Despite their delight, Larry wasn't sure when he'd visited these friends previously. That was probably because his memory was not as sharp as it used to be, a bit like the bright blue sky which seemed to have dimmed a little as time went by.

'It's a bugger getting old,' he said, to no one in particular. That was his favourite new saying and, though no one heard him, Larry didn't care.

He loved whomever he visited. And they always seemed to love him. He often wondered why. He wasn't anything special. He knew that. Maybe it was because he was good-looking and easy to get along with, he grinned.

He wasn't the world's biggest diner and he didn't think he was too fussy. He didn't like fruit and vegies, though. He preferred delicacies, things that the rest of civilisation seemed to detest or were too scared to taste.

'More fool them,' Larry said, once more to no one in particular.

Neither did he drink tap water; probably the chlorine had something to do with that. But he was fine with rainwater. Even filtered water would do.

These latest friends were really accommodating. They'd greet him every morning and say goodnight to him at bedtime. Other than that, they'd let him do his own thing. Most days he'd chill outside, taking it easy on their lush, neatly manicured lawns. Occasionally, he'd get on their lounger and soak up some sun.

That was the kind of R & R Larry desperately needed – and he was grateful for his friends' hospitality, especially as they weren't his favourite acquaintances. There were lots of other generous families who would've been more than happy to accommodate him.

As the summer months went by, Larry retreated into shadier spots in his friends' garden, especially on sweltering days. Even then, he found the heat intense. However, he didn't like to go inside to escape the warm temperatures because he and air conditioners got along as well as cats and goldfish in any family household.

It was time, he realised, to return home. His nearest and dearest would be missing him. Priscilla, his darling wife, might already have listed him with the local constabulary as 'gone missing'. That would have created a stir in his industrious community.

It was with a heavy heart that Larry decided to depart. He'd thoroughly enjoyed his stay, but it was time to move on. He hated teary goodbyes. He got too emotional and, if he was really bad, he'd sometimes be grumpy when he arrived home.

He wondered if he should leave a note. Then he remembered that although that would be a nice thing to do, it would not be possible for him to accomplish the task. No, he'd just remove himself…quietly, like a shadow disappears in dim light. His host and hostess would understand.

When the sun rose next morning, Larry whispered, to no one in particular, 'Look, it's been great,' he said. 'I've had the most wonderful time. I feel refreshed, ready to take on the world.'

Fighting back tears as he went on his way, he added, 'It's time to get back to my family, all of them…including my many baby lizards who, I've decided, will all be renamed Larry when I get back to the scrub.'

# See You Later

'That's it – I'm never doing this again!' Mrs Claus was adamant. For too many years, she'd had to bear loads as heavy as Santa's sacks on Christmas Eve. She'd had enough.

Her portly husband didn't flinch. He'd heard it all before.

After the big rush, Mrs Claus always felt this way. She was tired on so many levels: hours in their tiny kitchen baking for all those elves and reindeer; sitting at her sewing machine, making new red and green outfits and hats for all of the countless little workers; and, in their large workshop, labelling all the toys for the trillions of households around the world. All of this took its toll. And she wasn't getting any younger.

At the start of each year, she often threatened to call it quits. Yet, year after year, as the festive season drew closer, Mrs Claus always put the bigger picture before herself.

'The littlies will be over the moon again,' Santa reminded her whenever he felt his wife needed a little nudge to keep up her momentum. 'Think of all the wonderful memories those kids will be able to share with their brothers and sisters as they get older,' he added. 'Think of the tales, about the wonderful toys they've been lucky enough to receive over the years, that they'll be able to tell their children and grandchildren.'

He paused before a final tribute: 'And it's all thanks to us.'

They both knew it was emotional blackmail. But Mrs Claus had always relented. She was too kindly and considerate of others not to succumb.

This time, though, Santa was concerned. Mrs Claus had sounded as if she'd really meant it. What was he to do? He knew he wouldn't cope with the huge workload without her. She was the backbone of Santa Claus Inc. Without her aid, he was doomed – and so were all little kids around the world. And some big ones too.

But he had prepared for such a crisis. As with any smart entrepreneur, he had a plan for just such an emergency.

'You need a break, darling,' he told her. 'And I've got it all worked out for you.'

'What devious plan do you have in mind?' Mrs Claus asked. Though millions around the world trusted her husband, she knew better.

'At the end of the week, we fly out,' said Santa.

'To where?' she asked.

'The other side of the world.'

'Where exactly?'

'South Australia.'

'I've heard of Australia. Kangaroos and koalas, and flies as big as bats. And very hot days and bushfires.'

Mrs Claus was usually a half glass-full kind of person. She must be exhausted, Santa thought.

'Ah, there will be some wildlife where we're going. But we'll most likely view many of them in their natural habitat. You see,' Santa said, twirling his beard with the confidence of a master planner, 'we will be taking a short cruise.'

'To where?' demanded Mrs Claus.

'Kangaroo Island.'

'Where's that?'

'Very close to Adelaide, South Australia's capital city.'

So it was that Santa and Mrs Claus left the cooler temperatures of the North Pole to the heightened temperatures Down Under. Though it was a long trip, the pair slept soundly in their business-class seats, an upgrade provided by Virgin airlines, whose boss was a passionate fan of the big man and his wife.

Arriving refreshed, they quickly became inquisitive tourists. Mrs Claus was particularly enamoured by some of the state's unusual sights and merchandise which she'd seldom had the time to check out back home.

Her visit to the Buddha statue in Sellicks Beach was a highlight. She thought it majestic and serene, caressing the wide expanse of ocean like a lighthouse might.

As with other mothers, Mrs Claus always had time for shopping. IKEA's flat-packs tickled her fancy, though Santa thought of the countless hours he'd need to spend putting all the ins and outs together back home. He decided that would give the elves something to do in their less frenetic months.

They left Outer Harbor for the short cruise to Kangaroo Island, the zoo without fences. There they tasted local honey and cheeses, and did part of the wilderness trail, embraced lovingly by wildlife, towering gums and a coast unsurpassed.

Too soon, it was over and they were back in snug seats, heading home.

'That was marvellous, darling,' Mrs Claus told her husband, beaming cheeks ruddier than usual.

'My pleasure,' he said. Mission accomplished, he thought. She's recharged and ready to take on the world again.

He decided to make his move before the glow wore off. 'So you've had second thoughts about calling it a day, no doubt?' he said.

Mrs Claus smiled. 'Like I said, I've had the most wonderful time,' she told her husband. 'So wonderful that I've decided to retire so I can travel around the world in luxury for the rest of my life. And, if you'd like to, you can join me.'

# Scorched Veldt

Koos Venter kissed his wife, Ena, on her forehead. 'Night, sweetie,' he said, dropping his belt from around his thick waist.

It had been a long night for the overweight policeman and father of three adult boys. He hankered for the bed his wife had just vacated. The late night/early morning shift always got to him. It had been a quiet evening, but he was as weary as a young rocker just home after an all-night stint in a pub.

Of course, Koos wasn't that age any more. Those riotous nights he'd left to his sons, now strapping lads all in their twenties, and always, without fail, on the lookout for a good time with anyone, especially those they thought were fair game.

'You have a nice day, sweetie,' Koos told Ena as he stripped to his boxers.

After years of rearing their sons, his wife had gone back to nursing, her passion. That was where she was heading for her dayshift job at the local medical centre. The pair seldom caught up. They led busy lives, trying to lay their golden nest eggs for advanced years.

'See you later, honey,' she told Koos.

She turned back abruptly, brushing dusky lips against his left cheek. She longed to let them linger, then slide them towards his strong, rough mouth…but that kind of thing no longer happened. There were never enough hours in a day for either of them. And they were always exhausted.

'One day,' she said to herself as she walked briskly, car keys in hand, towards the front door, 'we'll get back to those days.'

*

Serafina opened the back door of the mansion in the centre of the affluent, white suburb. She earned her livelihood by maintaining the home for the family three times a week. On the other two days, Serafina ironed clothes for another white family close by.

However, for almost two years, the family from the mansion provided her with the money she needed to afford her tiny, one-bedroomed home at the base of the mist-clothed mountain an hour's train ride away.

Serafina proved to be a trustworthy servant to the busy couple with three grown sons. So dependable that, a year or so into her employment, they'd left her the back door key to enter their home. This kind of thing didn't happen often in their community and the 'master', as she called Koos Venter, had emphasised this fact.

'Madam is not happy for me to give you this key,' Koos told his servant. 'But I trust you, Serafina… I trust you,' he'd told her.

Quietly but thoroughly, Serafina had gone about her duties, which included cleaning, washing, steaming floors, food preparation, cooking, and when the 'master' awoke, vacuuming.

Serafina had loved her job and worked happily, usually in the solitude she preferred, for close on two years…until one afternoon, just as dusk was spreading its tentacles around the sleepy mansion.

She'd been gazing out of the kitchen window, contentedly stirring the curry she'd prepared for Koos and Ena Venter, and their three adult sons, who all still lived at home.

She thought initially she might have been daydreaming when, out of nowhere, from behind her, she felt two hands, bulky and strong, shift swiftly around her braless breasts…and hug her close.

Realising with suddenness this was anything but a dream, Serafina turned and, recognising the face in an instant, flashed her hands to her mouth in disbelief.

*

Serafina gazed through the mist which hugged the mountain range. She sat cross-legged in her sparse, dusty backyard, through which a restless stream flowed on its meandering path to nowhere. She wiped her forehead with a damp cloth. It was going to be another charring day. Just as all the days before it.

Sweat formed, then hurriedly dripped from her sculptured nose down into a mouth thick and sensuous. Sometimes, but no longer as often, her lips spread top and bottom to reveal teeth whiter than any toothpaste, a contrast to her body, forever bathed in charcoal.

She had a tiny, brown earring in one side of her nose and others, large and wooden, jangled from ears stretched from years of fitted over-sized adornments. Curly dark hair peeked out of the *doek*, a headdress, its shades no longer colourful. Instead, she chose grey, for her the hue of mourning.

As she rose to her statuesque height, Serafina paused. Carefully, she placed both hands on her midriff, gently rubbing the swelling which had, in recent months, enlarged like an unforgiving, unwanted cyst.

She hardly noticed the tear fall from one eye. The single drop fell to the ground, engulfed instantly by the ravenous dirt. She took the broom which rested idly alongside a dead plant, and swept away the leaves which had fallen from the *kaffirboom*. She swept them this way and that, that way and this, until she had them formed into a pile.

She wished her trauma could be swept away as easily.

It was time for work at the mansion.

Serafina shuddered at the thought.

# Lesson Learned

Quietly, in the numbness of night, Simon tiptoed into his father's bedroom. Simon knew his father, Ronaldo, was asleep. Snoring loudly enough to wake neighbours at the end of the street, Ronaldo, as usual, had consumed a couple of brandies before bedtime.

'It's my sleeping tablet,' he'd told Simon often, after Angelica – his wife and Simon's mother – had died in a road accident just a year ago.

'Sure, Dad,' Simon had told his still-grieving father earlier that night.

Angelica had meant everything to the pair. An only child, Simon had worshipped his parents, his bond with his dad becoming even stronger after his mother's death.

But there were two questionable characteristics Simon had inherited from his father. He was independent and stubborn. They were the reasons Simon was now in his father's room, fiddling for the prize in the pockets of his father's trousers, which rested over a chair at the edge of the darkened room.

Ronaldo always kept the keys to his Volvo in his pants pockets. 'I'll never lose them or not find them because they're always in there, even when I'm asleep,' he'd said.

Now, as Simon rummaged through the pockets, he sweated on the knowledge he was doing wrong. Recently turned seventeen, he was taking driving lessons – and was besotted. Steering a wheel had become his first and only love. He wanted to practise as often as possible. He also wanted to do so in his father's Volvo, not the hatchback his father used to drive to market twice weekly to buy vegies for his deli. Simon, courtesy of his father, used the hatchback for his driving lessons.

'Yes, you can use the hatch – no, you can't use the Volvo,' Ronaldo had told his son from the start.

'But, Dad…'

'No buts, Simon. Right now the Volvo is mine. You know it was handed down in the family. But it's also powerful. You're not experienced enough to drive that car.'

Simon had uncharacteristically sulked about that decision but his father was having none of it. Even then, Simon knew he would find a way.

Before treading into his father's bedroom that night, Simon had known Ronaldo would not rise early the next morning to go to market. He'd suspected, too, that Ronaldo had consumed more than his customary two drinks before going to bed. It would be the ideal time to make his move.

Simon soon felt the silver, serrated keys of the Volvo fitting snugly in his hand. As quietly as he'd entered, he exited his father's room. Within seconds, he had soundlessly shut the front door of their modest house and moved to the double-vehicle carport on the other side of the bedrooms.

The Volvo's engine purred as contentedly as a cat chewing on choicest cuisine.

Soon, Simon was out of the suburbs and on the open road nearby their country home. With windows rolled down to take in the fresh Spring air, Simon was cruising. He was the King of the Road, the Master of Metal, the Pride of the Tribe – and he was loving the ride.

Until he noticed them. In the review mirror. Two lights.

He tried to ignore them. 'I'm not the only person on this Earth with a God-given right to go cruising at three in the morning,' he heard himself say.

The longer he rode, the larger the vehicle behind him loomed. However, it kept the same distance away, whether Simon put a heavier foot to the metal, or slowed.

Panic turned to fear. He recalled stories about killers in the night on quiet, country roads. It was time to head home. Taking an alternative route was the best option, he decided. He'd been driving for forty minutes. The route back was shorter.

But the stalker shadowed.

Taking different streets hadn't helped. The lights followed, slow, sure – until Simon drove with care, the Volvo's beams off, into the carport.

He switched off the ignition, and turned to look behind him.

Down the road he saw the lights of the vehicle die too.

'Do I get out? Or do I stay in?' Simon's mind, seized by dread, whizzed like a washing machine blitzes on overdrive. 'Should I make a dash for it?'

He decided. Open the Volvo door slowly – and charge into the house. As he edged the door open, a figure from the other vehicle emerged.

'What you been up to, son?' asked his father.

*

Later, Ronaldo told his son it wasn't that Simon had taken the vehicle without permission which upset him. It was the fact that as an inexperienced driver, he'd put himself at risk.

'I've lost one precious family member in an accident – I don't want to lose another,' Simon's father said. 'And, by the way, just so you never forget this little lesson – not only will the Volvo be out of bounds, but I've taken back the hatchback keys and they'll be staying with me, in my pockets, day and night, for the next twelve months.'

# Sex, Lies and Videos

'Let go of me,' Fantasia screamed. 'Let go!'

Toby had her apron firmly in his mouth – and he was not about to let go. He wanted what she was baking and nothing would stop him trying to get at it.

Fantasia looked around for something that would discourage his annoying behaviour. Not finding anything suitable, she let him have it. 'Take that, you brat,' she said, catching Toby with solid kicks to his body.

That subdued him but not altogether. He came back for more.

This time, Fantasia collected Toby in the ribs. She was pleased she hadn't removed her working boots before coming into the kitchen.

'You're a bloody nuisance,' she shouted at him. 'Can't wait to get rid of you!' She let fly with her boots yet again.

As she did so, she realised, with trepidation, that someone had been watching. She turned quickly, but saw no one.

As she looked up, she saw a figure withdraw hurriedly from an upstairs doorway. Fantasia had no idea whom it might have been. The house had been crowded with cleaners before her big day. Most likely it was one of them, she decided.

*

Annabel darted back to her bedroom. She hated that woman, the woman who was to become her stepmother. How could her father do this to her? How could her father be in love with a woman named Fantasia, for God's sake? Worse still, how could he have proposed to that woman without consulting her, his only daughter?

The marriage had been hastily arranged. Annabel had been led to believe it was because Fantasia was pregnant. Or had told Sergio she was. He had to do the honourable thing and marry her even though Annabel was sure her father was not in love with that horrible, cruel woman. How could he be? He was in love with her one and only mother, the woman he had always loved, the woman who was no longer with them.

'Oh, Mum, I miss you,' she whispered.

Tears again came quickly. They had come swiftly and often since news of the accident which had killed her mother. The day her life came crashing down was the day she swore her father would never ever replace her dearest mother with anyone.

'Least of all someone called Fantasia,' Annabel said aloud.

She knew now, though, that she had found a way to thwart the marriage.

*

Fantasia was all set for her dream moment. It was a sunny day, similar to those flaunted in holiday resort presentations. Forecasts indicated it would stay that way. The house was spotless, the gardens trimmed to shape, the caterers had everything in hand. All that was left was for her to look beautiful, something she knew she'd find easy to do.

She and Sergio had agreed on the garden wedding, with just their closest friends. And, of course, the celebrant who'd bring them together.

Fantasia had admitted to herself long ago that she wasn't in love with Sergio, but she knew his wealth would ensure her happiness. That was all she wanted. She'd struggled for too long, doing housework for other people. Though that job had provided the chance for her to meet Sergio, she knew she'd never have to get her hands dirty again. Now, other women would keep her house looking as glamorous as she. As she held that thought, she smiled, delighted as a wife-to-be on her hen's night.

It was nearly time. Thirty guests were seated on chairs stained with an avocado tint and tied with gigantic, orange bows, Fantasia's idea of style. They watched as the bride walked down the navy carpet into an archway which peered out towards the ocean.

'Do you Fantasia take this man to be your lawful wedded husband?' read the celebrant.

Fantasia agreed to. So did Sergio when asked to take her as his wife.

Rather anxiously, as always, the preacher read out the words Annabel had been awaiting, 'Is there anyone here present who believes this marriage should not take place?'

At this moment, Annabel was elated she'd almost walked down into the kitchen two days ago when she'd heard the commotion.

She'd run her iPhone on video mode and had captured all of Fantasia's brutal attack on her father's favourite fellow. Once Sergio saw the video, she knew this mismatch would be over before it had started.

Nobody came between her father and his best mate of thirteen years, his one-and-only Toby, the only male on earth Sergio loved and trusted.

'Is there anyone here present who believes this marriage should not take place?' the celebrant repeated.

'I do,' yelled Annabel, waving her flashing phone above her head.

'Woof,' barked Toby, dead on cue.

# Family First

Peter Fitzgerald had spent many years of his young life foraging for food.

He recalled he was never told to go out and seek food for himself, for his siblings, for his parents. He just did. He had to – so he and his family could survive. He was, after all, the eldest of his brothers and sisters, and his father, who had been the breadwinner, was no longer capable of working since the mining accident had left him bedridden.

His father, who'd taught him so much about being strong and supportive of the family, sadly was no longer in a position to do as he'd preached. 'Don't care what you do with your life, son, but you've got to do it for your family – no matter what,' he'd told Peter. 'Your family comes first. Never you. Do whatever it takes to make life easier for your family.'

His dad's words echoed in his mind the first time Peter went scavenging. He recalled not being able to stand the pitiful cries of his starving brothers and sisters hours before he'd tiptoed out of the hovel which served as a house to seven people.

The back streets of eating houses were his first points of call – and he had immediate success. Leftover vegetables, raw and cooked, were scooped into the pockets of his father's old army coat which soon resembled bulging insides of pool table catchers.

The delight on the faces of his siblings at the sight of the scraps made all risks worthwhile.

He knew, as did his dad, that petty thieving – even taking goods from a garbage bin that didn't belong to you – was a crime. Though, at fourteen, he was young, Peter was aware, as was his dad, that if he were caught, the repercussions could indeed be grave for him and the family.

*

For more than three years, lanky, skinny Peter Fitzgerald supplied second-hand grub to his parents and his brothers and sisters. That supplemented the meagre few shillings the government had meted out to his ailing father.

One night, murky as a *Wuthering Heights* setting, Peter's luck ran out. So intent was the lad on stuffing his pockets with provisions, he failed to detect the burly copper turn the corner on to the pebbled road. The boy was handcuffed and holed up in jail before he had a chance to plead his case.

Justice in those days was swift and unbending. The lad who would be his family's saviour was sentenced as an adult – to five years hard labour in a colony far from his home country of Ireland.

That was a place called Van Diemen's Land.

*

It was a few weeks before Peter Fitzgerald would be bound for that new land and it was now, in a rotting jail, no better than a sewer full of rats, that he found himself as hungry as he had ever been – even hungrier than his days as a youthful forager.

Kitchen staff at the jail he was in had been on strike for more than a fortnight, and no prisoner had been fed during that time.

As Peter lay among hordes of other stinking, emaciated bodies, he closed his eyes and could think only of the last meal he'd had in that prison.

In those days – the 1830s – prisoners were usually given a spoon, a two-pint zinc dish for broth, and a tiny zinc bowl for milk. As it was winter, milk was in short supply and prisoners had had to settle for treacle water, weeks and weeks of treacle water. He was also allowed six ounces of bread.

For Peter, that last meal – before the cooks' strike – of greasy broth, complete with a sliver of ox head, a taste of barley, peas and leeks, as well as three-day-old bread, washed down with treacle water, was one that now had him salivating.

Ultimately, just the thought of that meal was enough to keep him going – even after the strike ended and he'd made it all the way to Van Diemen's Land.

On arrival, Peter was told he'd become the sole survivor of his immediate family. The family he'd spent many years of his life saving – and given his liberty for – had all perished in a house fire just before Peter stepped foot in the new country.

*

Years later, after becoming a free man, Peter moved to farmland on what later became known as the Eyre Peninsula. He met and married a Yorkshire lass and together they had a brood of children as healthy and robust as the oxen they farmed together.

To the day he died at the age of ninety-two, Peter's favourite meal was a thick broth, with slivers of ox meat, ample portions of barley, peas and leeks, accompanied by steaming hot damper caked in thick butter.

But there was never, ever, a drop of treacle water in sight.

# Karma Finds a Way

Genevieve Freud had a vivid imagination. Everyone told her mother that.

Even though she wasn't yet a teenager, Genevieve seemed to find herself in so many predicaments, her mum wondered if the slim, tiny, bespectacled child with plaited black hair was ever truthful. She was nothing like her other siblings who were…well, normal. Mrs Freud often wondered if she ought to take Genevieve to see a psychoanalyst as advised by her therapist.

Because of her oddness, Genevieve had only one friend, Bettina Jung, who lived next door.

Sadly, the girls' mothers didn't get along.

Genevieve's Mum detested Bettina's mother because she was sure Mrs Jung, many moons ago, had stolen her favourite lilac towel from their washing line at the back of her house.

Genevieve's mother was certain Mrs Jung had stolen it because she'd seen it on her line just days after it went missing. When Mrs Freud questioned her about the missing lilac linen, Bettina's mother said, 'Impossible – it's been our favourite towel for years.'

'Karma will punish that woman one day,' Mrs Freud told Genevieve at the time.

*

The girls continued to be friends despite this row between their mothers.

Mrs Freud was, at the time, more concerned about Genevieve's imagination, which kept getting her daughter into a pickle.

Her latest tale was a case in point. Genevieve related the story to her mother the morning after it had apparently occurred.

Genevieve had seen her latest spectacle emerge through her bedroom window by the light of the full moon, when the night was cloudless and the house so still not even her black cat emerged from its slumber to chase bats as was her usual nocturnal habit.

'I watched the figure dangling from the parachute as it came tumbling down, landing on our property just in front of the quarry,' Genevieve explained to her mother. 'I didn't want to wake anyone and I decided to follow in the general direction I thought the figure had landed. The moon was bright, the footprints easily seen.'

With a sigh, Genevieve's mother feigned interest in yet another of her daughter's tales.

'The trail went on for such a long time I thought of turning back,' continued Genevieve. 'I must have walked an hour when I came upon the parachute. It was piled up. Next to it lay a figure. I approached quietly and cautiously. I heard noises. Strange noises. Then I realised what they were. Somebody was snoring.'

'You're making this up, Genevieve – again.'

'I'm not, Mum. Do you want to hear what happened next?'

'Go on then, girl.' Despite herself, Mrs Freud was intrigued.

'I crept closer, making sure to tread carefully, not to break any twig which might awaken the stranger. I noticed his face was covered by what looked like a wooden mask.'

'I cannot believe you were out there alone near someone like that. Dear girl, he could have attacked you.'

'I told you, Mum, he was asleep and I was careful. I crept even closer and grabbed the large bag next to the parachute. Then I turned and ran back home.'

*

Holding the bag now, Genevieve opened it as if for the first time. She knew what was inside. She plucked it out, showing her mother.

It was an abacus.

'See. It's all true. Where else would have I got this from?'

'Is there anything else inside the bag?' her mother asked.

'I didn't check,' said Genevieve.

She shook the bag. A note fell to the floor. She unravelled it. She read it to her mother, whose interest had suddenly become more than just passing: 'The person into whose hands this ancient counting frame falls will in turn come into a fortune. However, you need to find the matching one to secure that fortune.'

'You've made this all up, Genevieve,' her mother, all bothered, said.

'No, but you know what this means, Mum? The other abacus must be in the vicinity. Why else would that person have parachuted on to our land? We must find it.'

*

A knock on the front door startled them. Mrs Freud peered through the curtained window. It was Bettina's mother, from next door.

'Hello, darling,' Mrs Jung said as Genevieve opened the door. 'Is your mother in?'

'No, she's not.' Genevieve lied, because her mother had told her to before she'd darted up the stairs.

'Well, when she's back, tell her Bettina told me about the garage sale you're having next week. I've got something in this bag your mother might want to sell for me – not sure what it's worth but I'm happy with whatever she can get.'

Genevieve thanked Mrs Jung, though she knew her mother wouldn't bother trying to sell the item for the woman she detested.

Genevieve opened the bag Mrs Jung had given her. Suddenly shaken, she dropped it. She stifled a cry.

Her mother, walking back down the stairs, saw the look of shock on her face. 'What is it?' asked Mrs Freud.

Unable to speak, Genevieve pointed at the bag.

Inside was a matching replica of the ancient counting frame.

# The Blue Silk Kimono

'What ya up to, mate?' Joe said, lounging on the sofa.

'What on earth do you mean by that?' Perrigren replied, grooming his eyebrows in a hallway mirror.

Joe was aware Perrigren had been in Australia for just a few weeks. Students, they'd found themselves sharing a space at the university's boarding hostel.

'I mean, what you been up to today, mate?' Joe replied, lifting his legs on to the wooden coffee table laden with cans. He cracked open another beer.

'Studying and more studying, old chap,' Perrigren replied.

He was good-looking in a Pommy kind of way. Not a hair out of place, Perrigren usually wore suits and ties, even to lectures. He'd already been mistaken once for a lecturer, which amused him a tad.

'Sloppy' Joe, as his room-mate was known to friends, couldn't have been more of a contrast. Footy shorts, T-shirts and thongs were his idea of fashion.

It's gonna be a tough year, Joe thought to himself, sucking on a rollie.

'Do you have to smoke inside, old chap?' Perrigren said. 'Bit inconsiderate of you, is it not?'

'No worries, mate,' said Joe, picking up his beer. 'I'll hit the outside deck and clear outta your way.'

A peace activist, Joe believed all goodwill started at home, and spread to the rest of the world from there.

Possibly due to their differences and largely because of Joe's relaxed nature, the pair, in their early twenties, became friendly. Six months on, they were best mates.

'Thought you were a right ponce the first time I set eyes on you,' said Joe during a lecture break.

'I thought you were the scabbiest person I'd ever seen, like the poor child of one of those outcasts deported from my homeland,' said Perrigren.

'Who calls their kid Perrigren?' Joe had responded.

They enjoyed each other's company and often drank together in pubs that tolerated diverse attires of dress. It was on one of these visits that the course of their liaison transformed forever.

Joe saw her first.

Perrigren reacted immediately. 'Strewth, she's flamin' gorgeous,' he said, as out of character as a dandy dresser without cufflinks.

The woman in the blue silk kimono was just that – all woman. Straight black hair cascaded to a slender waist and framed a face that was pale, accentuating high cheekbones. Sapphire-coloured eyes stood out like searchlights on a foggy night. Her lips made both men salivate – the brightest cherry-red lipstick begged to be kissed.

For both men, it was love at first glimpse. From the moment Sarika winked flirtatiously in the direction of the two friends on that first night, it was game on. She tantalised. She mesmerised.

She was also maddingly indecisive. One night it was Perrigren she fancied. The next it was Joe. She loved that they were so unalike. She thought often she would like to live with – and love – both men.

But they were having none of it. Neither was prepared to share this temptress. Both were smitten and wanted her all to himself. Having become firm friends, they were now confirmed rivals.

They were not to know the wickedness lurking behind the beauty.

*

Eventually, for the pair, there was only one way to end the dilemma.

Three months after meeting Sarika, the men agreed on an ultimatum.

'You've got to choose one of us,' said Joe.

'And whoever loses will be out of your life for good,' said Perrigren.

*

It was decided by the trio to meet at Sarika's spacious, modern studio. They arrived, attired to arouse – even Joe, always the slob, looked dashing in a tuxedo he'd borrowed, hoping to score last-minute brownie points.

Sarika had enticed the men to opposite sides of her large lounge room. She placed herself in the centre, but away from them.

It was like *High Noon* at nine paces.

Though the aircon was on, Joe and Perrigren were wet with sweat.

Sarika, dressed in the blue silk outfit that so stirred the duo on that first night, called them to attention. 'As you leave me with no choice, I'll keep this short and simple,' she said. She glanced at one, then the other.

She did so twice.

Three times…

'The man I'm choosing is…'

As the name of her chosen one lisped on the edge of her tongue, a masked figure darted into the room, firing one bullet from the gun in his hand.

One of her suitors fell to the floor. He was dead before he hit it.

'Oh, my God,' screamed Sarika, shrouding the fatally struck man with her blue silk kimono.

As her outfit flushed with the dark blood of the fallen man's fatal wound, she looked up at his still-shocked friend and rival, then cried out in the direction of the fleeing assassin, 'You killed the wrong one! You killed the wrong one…'

# Taming of the Dingoes

Red Riding was about to visit her dearest grandmother, who lived deep in a forest – and she was as excited as any young woman could be.

Unlike many children, Red had always liked her name. It reminded her of the red-cloaked child in that fairy tale about a little girl, her grandmother, and the woodcutter, who saved the fairer sex from a big, bad wolf.

Red, like her mother and her grandmother, was a kind and generous person. She was a new-age woman, just like those other two strong women in her life would have been in their eras. Red's mother had divorced her husband early on in their marriage because he could not cope with the realisation he'd wed a strong, self-confident woman.

Red's grandmother was as independent. She had stayed faithful to her husband of fifty years because that's what people of her era did. When her husband died, she decided to live in the forest, deep in the Northern Territory.

There were no wolves in her neck of the forest, but there were dingoes. Red's grandmother loved the wild dogs, because they, too, she felt, were fiercely independent. They also feasted on the pests around her: the kangaroos, rabbits and rats. That was the practical reason for having an affinity with dingoes.

But her empathy for them was about to be challenged.

*

Red got lost in the forest on the way to her grandmother, despite having a GPS in her recently acquired Golf GT.

'These things are bloody hopeless in the bush,' muttered Red, flinging the GPS on to the back seat.

Many hours later, with scratches and dents on her new car, Red knocked on the front door of the tiny house in the forest.

'Grandma, you there? It's Red. I've come to visit.'

Red was her grandmother's favourite grandchild. Red had always been keen on a chat from the moment she could talk.

And they agreed on most things, particularly dingoes. Red's grandmother had taught her all she knew about the dingo: how they were descended from semi-domesticated dogs from Asia; how they returned to a wild lifestyle when introduced to Australia; how they made their dens in deserted rabbit holes and hollow logs close to water; and how a dingo was once found to have taken the baby of a woman at a campsite not far from where she lived.

Arm in arm on their excursions, Red's grandmother would show her granddaughter the carvings of dingoes drawn on rocks in caves. 'Did you know, Red, that they're listed as vulnerable to extinction?' said Red's grandmother. 'And that's a pity. They're wild, but they're magnificent creatures.'

Her opinion was about to be tested.

*

The two women had just finished an end-of-day glass of wine from Red's grandmother's makeshift cellar when they first heard the sounds.

'Wooof, woooof, wooooof.'

'Sounds like a dog,' said Red, straight-faced.

'Whoo-ooo, whoo-ooo, whoo-ooo,' came more noises.

'Sounds like a howling dog,' said Red, still expressionless.

'Sounds like there're a few of them,' said her grandmother. 'Never heard that down these ways before.'

Soon, two or three howling dogs were joined by many more. Then there was another sound…the thump of animals tearing at the flyscreen of the front door of the little home. It was hardly a sturdy home. It seemed a huff and a puff might easily have blown the house down.

It was near dusk. Dressed in a hooded coat she often wore as a safety device, Red peered from the kitchen window. At least a dozen dingoes were tearing furiously at the wooden front door…barking, howling, panting, foaming at the mouth.

'Maybe there was some truth to that story about the woman losing her baby to a dingo in that camping ground,' said Red's grandmother.

Fearful but thinking clearly, the two women withdrew to the safety of the lounge, locking its door firmly behind them.

Soon there was another sound…a clear, wind-like whistle, a sound which seemed to soothe and comfort. It seemed to come from the heavens, wrapping the tiny house in its grasp as a caring mother en-velops a frightened child…a sound that also calmed the dingoes, which appeared drained from their exertions and withdrew into the shelter of the night.

There was a knock on the front door.

'Who is it?' shouted Red's grandmother, armed with her drained wine glass.

'It's me,' said a masculine voice.

'Who's me?' Red's grandmother responded.

'Shaun, the woodcutter,' came the reply.

*

As with others, this fairy tale has a happy ending.

Shaun, the woodcutter, became known in the forest as the Wild Dog Whisperer. He and Red fell in love and lived contentedly ever after. They also loved their jobs – Shaun, as a conservation and wildlife man-ager, and Red as a coordinator of a shelter for injured wild animals.

The three of them lived together, in the forest, in the not-so-tiny home (due to a bedroom and en suite extension), where Red's grand-mother worked, until she was no longer able to, as an animal rights ad-vocate, specialising in the welfare of highly-strung dingoes.

# Crushed Dreams

Samuel was in love with Nikita. It was weird that he felt this way. But not surprising. Samuel was different. Though eighteen, he was still a boy. He was skinny, of average height, with long, blond hair which he often tied up into a bun to keep the strands from his face. Especially when he read, which was often. In fact, he was referred to as the 'bookish boy' by most of his family.

Samuel was also an only child and often seemed bewildered in social situations, especially with children his own age. He was more comfortable with older people, and especially Nikita.

His mum would often frown when Samuel called Nikita by her name. That wasn't surprising either because Nikita was Samuel's aunt, his mother's twin sister.

*

'You're such a gorgeous boy,' Nikita would pronounce when she visited Samuel and his parents. She'd grab his ear lobes and tweak, then shake them from side to side as if trying to shift them from where they belonged. If anyone else did that, Samuel hated it. But Nikita could do no wrong.

She'd always insisted Samuel call her by her first name and not 'Aunty'. 'It makes me feel old when you call me that,' she'd told him.

Samuel liked Nikita because she lived up to her name. He considered it exotic. For him, it conjured up images of mystery. He thought it colourful, just as she was.

Nikita never dressed in the drab, black outfits worn by her twin sister. Instead, she tightly filled patterned dresses, usually matched with bright spectacle frames and a flower pinned to the side of her hair. She was always tanned, even in winter.

'It's fake, just like her,' Samuel's mother said.

But that didn't deter Samuel's feelings for his aunt. He thought she was a flirt, but that added to her charisma. She'd never married, but Samuel noticed men take lingering looks in her direction at functions with family and friends. Other women regarded her with suspicion and envy. But all the men, and boys of a similar age to Samuel, adored her. Statuesque, she flitted from group to group with energy and enthusiasm, with smiles which cheered the room, and laughter which sucked you, hungrily, into her world.

More than anything, Samuel loved her name. He Google-searched the meaning of Nikita. Greek origin, meaning unconquered, he discovered. It fitted her personality. No one would ever be her equal. She'd never be vanquished by any man.

Samuel had always loved how words suited their meanings, their images. Like the word 'voluptuous', which always reminded Samuel of a sumo wrestler.

*

The day the boy's world fragmented into splinters occurred forty-eight hours after Nikita had dropped in to wish Samuel's father a happy birthday.

'Can't stop for long, you lot, but had to pop in to wish you all the best,' she had said, plonking a gift onto Samuel's dad's lap. 'Have a wicked one – and see you all for lunch in a fortnight.'

She was there – and then she wasn't. Flit in, and out. Flit in, and out. In and out. Though she was no longer there, her presence continued to suffuse the space.

'Typical. It's always about her, when it suits her,' said Samuel's mum.

*

Two days later, Samuel walked home from school during mid-morning recess to pick up the science book he'd left behind. As he was about to open the front door, he thought he'd heard a laugh. He dismissed it. He reminded himself that his mum was at her part-time job as usual that day.

He noiselessly unlocked the front door. Inside, it had gone quiet. Or had it? Did he just hear sounds? Muffled sounds? Samuel thought he should retreat. Go back outside, a voice in his head warned. Instead, he took off his shoes. If there was someone in the house, he needed to tread as lightly as the turn of a page.

There was no one in the kitchen/dining area. He grabbed the umbrella leaning against the kitchen cupboard. He'd need it if there was an intruder. He decided to try the rooms leading off the kitchen. One by one, he told himself. Why did his mother always insist on closing these doors? Nothing in the first room. Nor the second. About to open the door to the third bedroom, he again heard a laugh. When he pushed open the door, confirmation of the sound hit him like a dagger to the heart.

The word 'voluptuous' suddenly reared into the forefront of his mind, but the image this time was not that of a sumo wrestler.

As naked as the time she'd skinny dipped in his parents' pool, when she thought she was alone, lay Nikita. With her on the bed, in nothing but his socks, was his father.

At that moment, Samuel's crush on his aunt died. Screaming, he fled the room.

# Home Truths

The little man lay there, sadly – his head severed from his rather fat body.

*

The shadow inside the home hurriedly drew the curtains, then as quickly opened them again. She did not believe what she could see. She hoped it was a figment of her latter years. That could not be Wilfred. Her precious Wilfred, the little man she'd brought from far, far away in her little hamlet in Windermere. At great expense, she'd had him transported from her abundant country garden so he could be with her in her new home until her time was up. She'd had Wilfred for more than thirty years.

'No, this cannot have happened,' she said one more time.

She quickly drew closed the curtains. She used her walking stick to shuffle toward her favourite chair, the one with the comfortable base. She needed it now she was getting on. A wisp of grey hair fell across creases of her face. There were no longer many wisps and she was grateful a few were able to curl out gravely from the frilly, faded bonnet she always wore.

She appeared much altered from the period when she was a high-spirited young woman who would make heads turn. In that lifetime, she would have had young suitors open doors for her, pull out chairs for her to sit in, or even lay down waistcoats so she could skip over puddles into the home she shared with her parents.

'Those were lovely times,' she said aloud.

She realised she was more alone than ever before. She had been alone for years since Vincent died. That was why she'd had to bring Wilfred to her.

'Wilfred?' she called again towards the curtain sheltering the window. 'Wilfred, was that you outside, without a head?'

There was no answer. She understood, after a while, she had not expected one.

She forced herself out of her chair. It took some time to shuffle back to the window. She stood there for some time. She realised she was in her night-dress. She wondered how long she had been in her sleepwear. Hours? Days? Weeks? Months?

'I don't want to think about that,' she admonished herself. 'I want to think about Wilfred.'

She recognised she could not remember what she'd had for breakfast that morning, but she recalled everything about Wilfred. She knew, for instance, he was the last remaining original.

'Probably because he killed all the others,' she said aloud. A smile creased her face.

She had spent almost all of the money her husband had left her to bid at auction for the man with the red pointy hat and matching shoes, blue shirt, and the wide brown buckle which secured long, black pants. And almost as much to get him to Western Australia, where she now lived.

He was made of clay, of course. Not like the wood, plastic, plaster, ceramic or metal ones that came later. He was her good luck charm. Besides adding a little whimsy and connection to the old world she remembered with such fondness, she always believed he would protect her from thieves and her garden from pests.

Lampy was his real name, but immediately he was delivered to her doorstep in the big box, tightly secured, she'd renamed him Wilfred. It had to be Wilfred because that was the name of the child she'd given birth to all those years ago, the child who had been stillborn.

The tears which slid down her face on to the bib she wore around her nightwear jerked her back to the present.

'I'll have to change this nightdress now,' she said.

She felt she would again be heartbroken once she opened the curtains and she saw Wilfred lying there, sadly, his head severed from his rather fat body.

Abruptly, she decided she would not be miserable because she realised at once what she would do when she again opened the curtains.

If Wilfred was lying there, with or without his head, she would take him to Gnomesville in the Ferguson Valley in Bunbury to be with the other seven thousand gnomes in the lush greenery, alongside the lazy stream curling its way through landscaped pathways.

He would be with his mates – the party gnomes, the plane-flying and john-sitting gnomes, even on occasions with those naughty gnomes in the fenced-in detention area.

Again, she drew open the curtains.

She smiled contentedly because she knew it didn't matter what Wilfred looked like, whether he was whole or disfigured.

'It's time for him to go,' she whispered. 'It's time for Wilfred to go to his new home in Gnomesville,' she said to the shadows, strange of shape, formed by the momentary rays of diminishing afternoon sun.

'Wilfred will be much happier there, away from me, away from this old woman who no longer can care for him, or herself…'

# Blow-ups

'Can't wait,' Jason said to himself. 'Birthday parties? This'll be a breeze.' He was as excited as a bucks' night bachelor. It was the first time he and his wife, Bethany, had decided to treat their five-year-old to a proper party with all the trimmings.

Small family gatherings had been the focus of Theodore's first four birthday celebrations. This time, however, most of his rather large pre-school class, and their parents, had been invited.

'Think you'll be OK with all this?' Bethany asked her husband, after informing him of the family's first foray into the precarious world of a full-blown kids' party.

'Too easy,' Jason said. Quietly, he relished this chance to show how much he'd matured since his drunken wedding day stoush with a grooms-man.

Bethany chuckled. She had an inkling they were words Jason might later regret.

Organised as always, Bethany had pre-ordered the food for delivery on the morning of the big day in question, and had mentally prepared the decoration of the tables with pretty trimmings and essential paper plates and plastic cups.

She'd left a note of things for Jason to tackle before, and on, the day. It wasn't a long list.

His first challenge was the balloons. Lots of shapes, colours and sizes. Jason tried the first. Five minutes later, drenched in sweat, he was still trying to fill the damn thing. Finally, it blew up in his face as he was about to knot it. Jason looked at the hundred and nineteen others languidly awaiting his heavy breathing. He knew there'd be no pub with his mates that arvo.

'You OK, honey?' Bethany asked.

'No probs,' Jason replied. Silently, he cursed this intrusion into his social life.

The next afternoon, they arrived in their hordes – kids, like the balloons, of all shapes, colours and sizes. Ditto their parents. Squeals of laughter and merriment soon turned their ordered home into an amusement park. When the grub came out, the guests tucked in.

As the presents were unwrapped so, too, did blow-up number two.

Theodore, usually a caring and compassionate child, abruptly became a total stranger, a person demonised. He kept close at hand every gift he'd been given that afternoon and refused to share a single present with anyone.

Soon, kids were screaming because they'd been denied the right to play a while with the gifts they had presented. Parents yelled loudly in an attempt to maintain discipline and restore order. Sounds similar to a bidding war in a New Delhi marketplace filled the air.

'You OK, honey?' Bethany asked Jason on her way to a rushed loo stopover.

'All good,' Jason replied. Quietly, he wished it was still acceptable to use a cane just like in the good old days when he was a kid. Just one cane. Just one little brat. And he'd reinstate serenity.

Rather than a restoration of tranquillity, however, parents were becoming more strained trying to secure a semblance of control.

Blow-up number three lurked.

Fuelled by copious amounts of beer and too-big glasses of bubbly, it wasn't long before they, too, crossed swords. Their focus shifted from their children to more grown-up conflicts. Discussions grew heated as they debated the best age to start birthday parties for their tiny monsters, questioned how much was too much to spend on these special occasions, and almost came to blows when weighing up the pros and cons of surprise parties for adults.

'You OK, honey?' Bethany asked.

'All's well,' replied Jason. Silently, he fumed as he placed flagons of water on tables, hoping to sober up all the disgusting mum-and-dad strangers before they decided to call it a night.

Finally, at nine p.m., seven hours after the party for a solitary five-year-old child began, Bethany and Jason once again took ownership of their home.

Their night, however, was not quite done.

Theodore, three hours past his usual bedtime and out of control following a diet of sugar for almost an entire day, buzzed around the house. He shot fake bullets from a plastic gun, climbed settees and chairs in his quest to escape the baddies, and finally screamed like a child possessed when he slid off his new skateboard and smacked face-first into one of his father's unsuspecting shins.

Blow-up number four was about to pounce.

'Just take him to his room and put him to bed,' Bethany said.

'No, you do it,' said Jason, replying before reflecting.

'What the hell happened to "too easy, no probs, all good, all's well"?' Bethany responded, her voice raised as high as her blood pressure.

'I said, you do it,' Jason replied, past the point of rationality.

'Get stuffed!' said Bethany. 'And once you're done putting him to bed, the spare room's all yours,' she said, slamming shut their bedroom door with the strength of Xena, the warrior princess.

'Birthday parties!' Jason yelled. 'More like a bloody typhoon than a breeze,' he added. 'Never again!'

# Paradise Lost

As he lay in the sand, his outstretched limbs tethered in all directions, Jackson Price laughed. It wasn't a happy sound. It was more like an hysterical cry.

And that wasn't surprising. Ants, as large as grasshoppers, crawled over his body. He was as trapped as a spider in honey. He knew there was no way out. Firmly bound, he wondered again how he'd managed to find himself in this position.

His thoughts were disrupted by a shattering, roaring sound. He strained his neck into an upright position. What he saw frightened him like nothing before. Now he knew for sure he had no chance.

'Get away, get away,' he screamed.

Then, Jackson Price blacked out.

*

Before the misfortune which had befallen him, Jackson's holiday of a lifetime had been just that.

Adventurous types, he and girlfriend Elana had surrendered themselves to the embracing tentacles of an African safari. They had seen wildlife up so close they could scarcely believe their good fortune. Herds of springbok, zebra and giraffe were common. Rhinos were always prominent. And birds they'd never seen before flew in for their daily swigs in a pond just metres from their bungalow in the midst of the bush.

Into the fourth week of their five-week tour, their hearts had been captured by the magic of Nature.

'I could die now and be forever happy,' Jackson told Elana.

They were words which tempted fate – and that was always dangerous.

*

On yet one more early morning tour, Jackson – mesmerised by the
splendour of his surroundings – had separated from Elana and others
on the tour.

He found himself encircled by another group, none of whose faces
he recognised. This group's members were nothing like the ones he'd
befriended. Whereas his tour guides carried rifles for protection, these
six held their weapons for an altogether different purpose.

All poachers, they were out for the kill. If strangers happened upon
them, they were happy to have their fun with them, too. These were
evil men, most of whom were born and bred into the world's wildest
jungles, before realising there was big cash to be made in more comfortable surrounds.

'What we do with white man?' the group's apparent leader asked.
He had a silver bandana strapped around thick, black, curly hair.

'I got idea,' said the leader, without waiting for a reply.

The others probably had an opinion, but assessed it in their interest
to let the boss decide on everything.

'We leave him for bait.' He laughed. That, too, was not a happy
laugh.

'No, let me go,' yelled Jackson. 'I'll walk away and tell no one about
you, tell no one anything…that this didn't happen.'

'You think we stupid, man?' the leader asked. 'You think wrong,'
he answered immediately on behalf of his captive.

Not long after, Jackson found himself lying in sand, his limbs tied
in all directions.

*

When Jackson regained consciousness after blacking out, his situation had altered.

Not for the better.

The roaring sound he'd heard before blacking out was that of the king of the beasts. It was time for a snack and Jackson presumably was in good enough nick to be on the menu. Jackson, still tethered, lay there.

The lion was in the mood for merriment. Jackson's eyes were closed, but he felt the lion's tongue, as rough as the back of a hedgehog, lick sweat off his skin, lick those ants as big as grasshoppers off his skin. The big cat was toying with him like a moggy jousts with a mouse.

Jackson guessed this lion once would have been in captivity. It had been tamed at some stage. It did not immediately go in for the kill as any lion in the wild would have. It wouldn't be long, however, before the lion would tire of the game.

Jackson suspected his holiday was about to conclude with an unhappy ending.

It was time for a proper feed. As the giant animal stood back, primed for his main course, Jackson shut his eyes again.

He tried to think how he could have avoided his predicament. He thought of his family, of his beautiful girlfriend, Elana, of all the people with whom he had crossed paths during his life's journey. He also tried, one more time, to think of some way he could get out of the mess he found himself.

Instead, he found himself pleading. 'Jesus,' he screamed. 'Jesus, please help me, please save me.'

Ignoring the strange sounds from his intended meal, the lion flew at Jackson Price, still lying in the sand, his outstretched limbs still tethered in all directions.

As the giant beast soared through the air, a single shot from a .22 rifle shattered the silence.

# Ageless Affair

'So, you had a worthwhile trip, Fran.'

'Worthwhile for you, Lizzy.'

'I ought to go with on your next jaunt.'

'That would get the journos salivating, Lizzy. They'll call for your head.'

'What's new, Fran? That Scottish waif, Mary, she who thinks herself a queen, has been calling for that for years.'

Francis didn't like it much that Elizabeth called him Fran. But he didn't want to offend the Queen of England – and he knew his knighthood was imminent. He would do whatever was needed for that dream to become a reality. If that meant he had to put up with Elizabeth calling him Fran, so be it. It was a term of endearment, sort of.

Elizabeth did not like to be called Lizzy. Especially by someone she believed was very much below her station. Francis, however, had done well to capture those six warships and sinking more than thirty others was more than a jolly good show, she felt. Besides, she loved the silk, spices and gold he brought home, especially for her.

She fondly fingered the white gold pendant, surrounded by twenty glittering diamond studs he'd presented to her when he'd arrived that morning. It was so stunning she'd disrobed immediately, without any aid from those bothersome maidens in waiting. Elizabeth liked to take her clothes off – they were, after all, uncomfortably heavy – and Francis had watched with a keen eye as she slowly and carefully rid herself of her many layers.

*

Francis thought back to the first time he'd realised there was a chance he and Elizabeth might get together for a royal to-do.

They were seated around the oval desk in the War Office with most of the influential members of the Royal Navy. He was briefing the Queen about his next conquest on the high seas.

He knew Elizabeth always had been attracted to naval officers. He knew also that though she was labelled the Virgin Queen by the press corps, she wasn't shy around men. He knew of two officers who had had their way with her, even though both had denied any shenanigans between royal silk sheets.

He recalled catching Elizabeth's eye in the War Office meeting while he revealed his plans to her with suitable deference. The attraction was instant. And electric. A torrid clash of eyes and colours, emerald and ruby, his and hers – and both were smitten.

Francis had not been surprised when, later that night, he was summoned to Elizabeth's boudoir. He was a bit shaken to see that, as soon as he'd arrived, she'd dismissed her maidens and, within seconds of their hasty retreats, she'd quickly dispensed of her elaborate gown and crown.

Francis was certainly not reminded of any hourglass when, mouth agape, he saw what the Queen did nothing to hide. He did remind himself, however, that there were never shades of grey when it came to those women he chose to annex. He'd always preferred busty and lusty – and Elizabeth certainly fitted this category.

After they'd partaken, with strenuous delight, of their respective titbits on offer and Francis was called to rather more serious matters of state, Elizabeth had pondered if he would be the man to help her ensure the continuation of the Tudor line for years to come. He's smart, he's dashing, he's got an eye for gold, she mused. Yes, he could be the one, she declared to herself.

*

Months passed, their relationship surviving the ebbs and flows of a couple who could not be seen in public together. That just wouldn't do, Elizabeth had thought. She was the monarch. Francis, though a Royal Navy officer, was a mere man, she felt, unashamedly. The longer the affair went on, however, the more daring the Queen became.

'I'm going to board your vessel,' said Elizabeth, after another night of passion.

'You usually do,' Francis responded.

She laughed, liking that about Francis. His sense of humour always delighted her.

'I've decided to present you with your knighthood aboard your ship,' she'd clarified.

'Is that not setting a precedent, Lizzy?' he'd asked.

'There's a first for everything, Fran.'

'But…but people will suspect.'

'I'm sure they do already,' she'd said.

*

So the day arrived in April 1581 for Lizzy to bestow on Fran one of his country's greatest honours. Amid much pomp and thousands of witnesses around their enchanted land, Queen Elizabeth I told Francis Drake, who was on bended knee with the sword of his beloved placed on her lover's shoulder, to 'Arise, Sir Francis.'

Which he did.

As usual.

## Footnote

History will dispute this tale as fantasy, and the following assertion, too: Lizzy and Fran lived happily together, out of wedlock, until an old age, among their brood of thirteen illegitimate children, some of whom may have become monarchs in their own right, centuries later.

# Brotherly Love

She'd told him to do it. So how could he refuse?

Simon had been wanting to do it for a while, but when Adriana had suggested that was the only way he'd get ahead, Simon knew he'd been right all along.

He had to find a way to get rid of his brother.

Simon had realised long ago he'd hated his perfect older brother. He hated him because his parents had loved him more. His brother also was better-looking, better at any sport they played, and far smarter than he was.

And his name conjured up a sense of a romantic past far removed from the present. His brother's name was Banjo. Everyone – friends and foes – was attracted to Banjo like mosquitoes to plump veins.

Only when Banjo was involved in a car smash did things change.

*

When Simon met Adriana nine months before the car accident, he was drunk. She was a model at the Melbourne Cup. He was on a promo jaunt for his financial company. He'd attended so many in the years he'd been employed that he was tiring of them, which was surprising. Simon never seemed to weary of the alcohol that flooded such functions.

'Bloody gorgeous you are,' he shouted at Adriana as she walked past him in the marquee tent.

She'd responded unexpectedly. 'True,' she'd told him. 'Pity you're not.'

Simon had always accepted rejection as a challenge. Adriana was worth the test. She was stunning. Simon never usually fell for brunettes.

But Adriana's mane was lush, thick and teased, tied up to a bun on top of her head, yet long enough to cascade down either side of her tanned face. Set up against black eyes – which growled at you when she was angry – and dense, black eyebrows, she was the flamenco dancer who fascinated.

He traced her mobile number, then hounded her for months before she gave in and went on a date. They'd clicked from the start. Soon, they became an item.

It had surprised Simon that she'd finally agreed. She was hot property. And never short of admirers. He'd never worried about any of them. But he was concerned about Banjo, the perfect brother he'd learned to hate. He'd never mentioned him to Adriana because he knew she'd be impressed once she set eyes on Banjo.

Strangely, when they did meet, she seemed indifferent. 'Too perfect for me,' she'd told Simon when they discussed his sibling.

'Good to hear,' said Simon.

'It's you I fancy,' Adriana said. 'However…'

'Yes?' said Simon.

'We need to get rid of him.'

*

The plan the pair hatched was simple. Simon would tamper with the brakes on the car Banjo drove. Banjo was always a high-speed driver. He'd wipe himself out.

Their terminally ill mother, who had just six months to live, had earmarked the family's riches to be shared between both brothers soon after her husband had died five years ago. Instead, with Banjo out of the way, that would all go to Simon.

Maybe, mused Simon, Banjo was not as smart as everyone thought.

*

News of Banjo's death was what he expected the morning after he'd tinkered with Banjo's car.

'It's terrible,' his mother cried into her phone. 'Your brother, your brother…'

'What, Mum? What about him?'

'He's been in car crash.'

Simon wanted to scream, 'I know, I know.' Instead, he said, 'Is he OK?'

'No. They've taken him to the hospital. Both legs have been crushed. They're talking amputation…'

'I'll be there as soon as I can,' said Simon. He switched off his phone. He turned to Adriana. 'Shit,' Simon said. 'He didn't die.'

*

Three months after the crash, Banjo was still alive, but without legs. He'd told police the accident occurred when he'd lost control going round a sharp bend and smashed into a big gum.

Because of his condition, medical expenses were vast. Much of the money set aside for the boys had gone. If there was anything left after Banjo had settled into a modified home, it would be minimal.

Driven by guilt, Simon changed. The brothers spent much of their time in rehab, Simon driving Banjo to make daily improvements.

Adriana grew bored. She realised money from this relationship would not change her life. She was also smart enough to realise that any attempt at blackmail would draw her into an attempted murder trial. She'd be accused of being an accessory. It was time for new ventures.

Simon, already accustomed to her superficiality, accepted her departure with minimal fuss. His focus was now on his brother. But he still drank heavily.

One night, after sculling Jim Beams like they'd soon be off the market, he'd told Banjo he'd fiddled with the brakes before the crash.

'I know, Simon,' his brother said. 'I knew it was you all along…'

'But you told police a different…'

Banjo cut him short. 'You're my brother. I suspected she'd put you up to it. I knew she was only after the cash. I also knew she'd get rid of you when there wasn't any.'

Simon hugged his brother, a human being more perfect than he had imagined.

# To Be or Not to Be

Hero Bugg had decided he was going to be something other than what he was destined to do on planet Earth. He wasn't going to be just a run-of-the-mill mate for her who rules. No, he was going to be something special. He would become king of the castle, sit on a throne, on his own, with no queen – and watch workers do all the hard yakka.

*

Hero was born to copulate – one of those sex objects who'd fly off with a queen of the clan, mate with her and…die.

As with all mates, he'd be alive for just a single season of passion. That, decided Hero, was ridiculous.

Queens could live up to thirty years. Workers – also female – survived for up to five years. Mates lived just for that one season. Totally unfair, pondered Hero, who was different from most other male mates, in that he had a brain. He could think. And he thought this tribal business had a lopsided hierarchy, disproportionally weighted in favour of females.

Frankly, Hero was a male chauvinist. And proud of it. So proud, he was determined to change the way males were recognised in the pecking order. Why did there always have to be a queen? Why couldn't a king rule?

Hero envied the life of a queen. She developed wings and flew out of nests to have her way with winged mates. After satisfying her lusts, she shed her wings, built a chamber or two in nesting spots, laid eggs, fed her young with her saliva and, for a light snack, absorbed unneeded wing muscles.

Easy life, thought Hero – basically, thirty years of sex, pregnancy and producing babies. Just not fair, he'd decided.

Granted, admitted Hero, other females in the colony were as busy as ticking clocks. Many kept the same job all their lives but most changed roles. Some gathered food for the colony and stored what they'd harvested in special chambers in nests. Some fed and cared for the queen and her young. Others built chambers and tunnels, using their saliva to harden the dirt walls. Some were soldiers, defending nests or using their large heads to block entrances to the nests. In short, thought Hero, most female workers had a lovely time – lots of variety and job satisfaction.

And males? Mostly, concluded Hero, they were used for their bodies. Off on a nuptial flight with their queen and, once the job was done, that was it for the studs.

Hero had decided he'd had a gutful. He knew he wouldn't mind the fun bit, but it was unfair he should be punished with death, merely for doing his job.

He opted to call a meeting of all other males. Obviously, it was to be discreet. He'd found a chamber no longer used by the queen.

'Guys, we need to stand up to these women,' he urged the dozen or so followers who also had a brain but who struggled to keep their seats. 'They've ruled the roost for too long – it's time we changed the world. Are you game?'

Amid the silence, scurrying sounds could be heard, but Hero continued, 'The plan is this: without us, the queen is buggered. She needs us to have kids. Without our mating skills, she's a goner. So, what I'm telling you is this: you need to say "No"!'

Hero heard a murmur of discontent. That soon became a chorus.

'But I don't want to die a virgin,' yelled one potential suitor.

'I've heard it's fun while it lasts,' screamed another.

'I'm doing it for my colony,' was a third response.

'Well, it looks like I'll have to go it alone,' Hero told the mates, now dwindled to a dribble. 'I'm going to stand up to the queen and be a man. I'm going to say "No"!'

*

Words, as we know, are easier said than deeds done.

When the time came for Hero's flight of fancy with the queen, he was left with no doubt he was to be the Chosen One. All her guile would be exercised on the handsome, clever rebel this trip, she'd decided.

Would Hero be able to withstand her charms?

Would he become something other than an object, to be toyed with at will?

Would the life he'd chosen for himself – free from sex – be the outcome?

Would he, in fact, become the first king of a colony?

Sadly, for Hero, none of these scenarios were able to be tested.

Sometime during the nuptial flight, Hero was set upon by other mates, also on the flight. These rivals had decided – at their own secret meeting – that Hero would not be the Chosen One.

Instead, he became the Evil One, the one who should be killed before he'd messed with the minds of all mates and spoil what, for them, was rightfully theirs.

Unhappily for Hero Bugg, the tribe had spoken.

# The Penfriend

Finally, it had arrived – the letter from Poland. Stella Beckley had waited so long for it, so many years; now at last, it had come. She'd thought her friend had gone forever. But now, she was here. In spirit, for the moment, at least.

Stella had been barely able to wait for the postman to deliver it. She'd kept watch from the window of her unit, almost as tiny as a doll's house, and had dashed out as soon as the postman had placed the letter in her sombre suede post box. Smothered in Polish stamps, the letter was postmarked two weeks ago. It didn't feel heavy, possibly containing only a page or two, but Stella didn't care. At least there was a letter.

Indoors, hands shaking, Stella took the letter opener from the mantelpiece. As she slid the sharp edge along the ridge of the envelope, she recalled how she and her friend had connected all those years ago…

*

'I've always wanted a penfriend,' Stella, just turned sixteen, said to herself in her bedroom, her fountain pen hovering over the flat map of the world on her desk. As she circled the pen in the air, Stella put up her left hand to cover her eyes. Then she let the pen drop.

'Krakow?' she said as the instrument landed. 'Where's that?' She peered at the map, searching for the name of the country in which Krakow appeared. 'Poland. Hmm. Don't know much about that place.'

Stella was a motivated young girl. Once she'd made up her mind about something, she immediately set to work. She was sure about this. She'd wanted a penfriend. Someone, far away from Australia, somewhere in Europe.

When her pen, with a nib as sharp as a needle, nearly smudged away the country of Poland on her faded map, she started on her mission.

Stella soon discovered the names of schools in Poland, then wrote several letters. Within a month or two, she'd received one reply, dated 6 April 1937. The English was poor, broken, but Stella was charmed by the sentiments of her new penfriend, Halina Bakowski, fifteen, also a final-year student at a school in Krakow.

In monthly letters to each other over two years, Stella and Halina formed a bond. Stella told her new friend about the wonderful things in Australia – the space, the weather, the lifestyle. Halina wrote to Stella about her country and, particularly, Krakow – its cultural treasures, architectural monuments, and its cobbled streets. They promised to visit each other – sometime, once they'd finished studying.

War, however, intervened. Letters between the girls became scarcer as conflict raged. Stella feared her friend would be lost as European countries succumbed to the Germans. She continued to write but most letters came back with UNDELIVERED – RETURN TO SENDER written across the front.

At war's end, in 1945, more than six million Poles had died. Stella never believed Halina was a victim and one story in particular gave her hope. It read that Polish children had been kidnapped in a project to take them from their country and moved to Germany to indoctrinate them into becoming culturally German. Stella hoped Halina would have been one of those. Better to be kidnapped than to be killed, she'd thought. She felt Halina would have been strong enough to cope with any brain-washing.

The years passed – ten, twenty, thirty, forty, fifty…

*

Stella's hands still shook as she clasped the cleanly slit envelope which the postman had just delivered. The letter opener dropped silently on to the thin carpet. Stella had had so few friendships in her life, so few people she knew or trusted. She'd never married. Her parents had passed on years ago and she'd had no siblings. She'd found a job as a clerk after the war and now, at sixty-eight, was relatively content in her retirement.

Unexpectedly, a telegram had recently arrived from Poland, which told her to expect a letter from someone – 'in the name of Halina Bakowski'. Stella recalled the feeling of dread when she'd received the telegram, then the excitement she felt at the news of an impending letter, possibly from her long-lost penfriend.

With fingers trembling like those of a soldier handed a loaded gun for the first time, Stella withdrew the letter from the envelope. She'd noticed, just then, the words Air Mail, in bright blue, stand out prominently on the light blue envelope.

Stella's name and address had been written in stylish black ink, all neatly set left, on the envelope. The letters were capitalised. Folded neatly inside was a single, wafer-thin page. On it were words written in cursive, all within two sizeable paragraphs. Stella read them both. Once, twice, then one more time. As she finished reading the paragraphs for the third time, a tear trickled sluggishly down towards her mouth, which quivered as if she'd just been struck by an intense fever.

Stella suddenly clutched the page to her chest – and sobbed.

# Village Mystery

They were found in the mud, only metres from the scene of the so-called crime. They were, of course, caked in dirt and grime, the village having being subjected to days of rain since the unholy deed was alleged to have occurred near the town's only phone box.

Would this help solve the mystery that had the local constabulary scratching heads with the futility of it all?

*

It hadn't taken long for the village to find out what had supposedly happened. It was, after all, only a tiny town, south of London.

Old Thelma McGuiness somehow got to hear of the alleged violation first. Once she'd found out, the gossip spread like a Zika virus through the village.

'Yes, I think I know who did something to Leonore Daintree,' Thelma told Angus Goodfellow, the skinny, gawkish police constable who had approached the old woman for a statement. He hadn't been happy that the village busy body apparently held a few aces in this investigation.

'And who would that be, Thelma?' Constable Goodfellow asked.

Thelma didn't like it that the young constable called her by her first name. She thought it showed scant respect for a clever and sensible woman such as herself. 'For me to know and you to find out, me lad,' said Thelma. 'I'm not here to do your dirty work for you, laddie.'

'By law, should you know, Thelma, you have to tell me.'

'Well, I ain't telling – not yet anyway, not till I do me own digging for clues.'

'I'll take it then that you haven't the slightest idea,' said Constable

Goodfellow, shaking a head of short-cropped black hair, his face dwarfed by that unwelcome family trait – a nose almost as long and thin as his police belt.

'That's where you're wrong, laddie,' said Thelma. 'Just wouldn't be fair to the bloke I suspect, specially if it weren't him.'

Constable Goodfellow rubbed his ample snout.

'I might be nosy – but I'm not a dibber unless I know for sure,' said Thelma. 'It just ain't fair.'

*

Leonore Daintree, meanwhile, the victim of the alleged offence, was in the office of Simon Lockwood, the district's inspector of police.

''Twere disgusting,' said the blonde. 'One minute he was walking towards me, by the village phone box, smiling a gobful of gums – this sad, sad man with no teeth – walking towards me, fully clothed – the next thing he was fiddling with his…his zip – the zip of his pants.'

'So you had a good look at his face, then?' asked Inspector Lockwood.

'Don't know about that,' said a piqued Miss Daintree. 'Just noticed his mouth, that he had no teeth, none at all, in his gob, like I said. And he weren't a local.'

'What exactly was he doing with the zip then, Miss Daintree?' Inspector Lockwood asked, trying to be patient.

He was tired. Exhausted, actually. Only ninety days to go and I'm out of here, retired for good, he told himself. Thirty years in the force had worn him out, worry lines altering a once-handsome face into a maze of furrows.

'I shan't say what he was doing with that zip – a lady would never repeat what she saw. It was too…too…horrible.' Miss Daintree's thick mascara started to run, along with a tear drop, down one of her rouged cheeks.

Inspector Lockwood sighed audibly. He knew Leonore Daintree

was known to have an unsavoury reputation in their little community, but it was never fair to judge people on hearsay. Despite his exhaustion, he remained a decent cop.

'I need to know the exact details, Miss Daintree. You say you were affronted, but I need to know how.'

Miss Daintree looked at the experienced inspector with large blue eyes which protested her plight. 'Use yer imagination, Inspector,' she said and turned away, shaking her blonde locks, only slightly shorter than the tight, black miniskirt she'd worn today and most other days of the week.

*

Inspector Lockwood and Constable Goodfellow sat miserably, eyeing each other over yet one more steaming, black dose of caffeine.

This was the biggest incident in the village for more than a decade – a local lass possibly indecently harassed. They had nothing, not a single clue, their prime witness, the victim, steadfastly refusing to add any additional information to her previous discussion with the inspector.

Suddenly, old Thelma McGuiness burst in, yelling triumphantly, holding aloft what appeared to be a possession to be prized. 'I found them, I found them,' Thelma screamed.

The two men shot off their chairs as if they'd both been stung in their posteriors by a cluster of wayward bees.

'In the mud, near the scene of the crime, right by the phone box, I found them,' Thelma continued to shriek about the event, later to be remembered in the annals of small village crime as the Case of the Missing Dentures.

# Floral Tribute

When I looked out from the kitchen window at my garden and saw those daisy-like, bright pink flowers I knew as the pigfaces, the memories came flooding back…

*

Mum would've been fifty the day it happened, the day I nearly lost Christabel.

I was in my mid-thirties and enjoying life as a stay-at-home mother. My daughter, Christabel, was the world's most beautiful little girl. I know all mothers think that about their children, but Christabel was just the most gorgeous toddler – easy-going nature, curly blonde locks like you see in those old films, and eyes the hue of a bright sky.

I'd always thought I'd want to go back to work soon after my first child was born, but I kept delaying my return. I'd run way past my maternity leave before deciding to go back. Even then, it was reluctantly.

I was lucky to have Mum. She'd always said she'd lend a hand whenever I decided I wanted to go back. Somehow, though, with Alan gone, I just felt I owed it to my beautiful daughter to stay home…as if I had to make up for her father, the man who never cared, the despicable human being who walked out on his wife and baby daughter just months after she was born.

I'd been devastated, I remember. Had it not been for Christabel and Mum, and of course Silver, I would never have survived the shock of Alan just leaving us all like that…not leaving a note…not explaining why…just leaving…just leaving…

And to think I nearly lost Christabel, too. The day *that* happened was one I remember more clearly than the day Alan left.

I think Alan's leaving was so out of the ordinary that for ages I felt it had happened to someone else, not to me. It was a blur for a long time, like the haze after a bushfire. People talk about out-of-body experiences. That's what it felt like for me.

But the day I nearly lost Christabel…

I remember Mum had come in early so I could get off to work. After Alan left us, Mum had always encouraged me to go back to my job so I could be among friends and colleagues at the hospital. She had been a nurse too, and she knew the camaraderie would be good for me.

So, despite my misgivings, my fear of facing everyone, of expecting everyone to point a finger in my direction and shout out that my husband had walked out on me, it was never like that. I was welcomed back warmly and genuinely. Mum was right, it was good for my well-being.

It got me back on track again – until that day I nearly lost Christabel, too.

I recalled the phone call.

'Darling, get back home. *Now.*'

It was Mum. It was her, but it sounded nothing like her. She'd never commanded, never demanded, not in that tone of voice. I did not question her insistence. Looking back, I think I'd been too scared to ask, in case it involved Christabel, in case I lost Christabel, too. I wouldn't have survived that.

When I arrived home, Mum was sitting on the veranda. Alone.

'Christabel… Mum, where is she…Christabel?'

It had been a frantic thirty-minute ride through traffic to get home – our quiet, little home in the middle of nowhere, kilometres away from anywhere. In the rush to my car, I'd left my mobile phone at the office. I'd been stressed. More stressed even than when Alan…pull yourself together, and ask the question I'd told myself.

Mum seemed dazed, in shock.

'Mum. Christabel?'

'She's fine. Inside. She's settled. Asleep. But Silver's not.'

Reassured beyond any other disquiets to hear my precious daughter was safe, I didn't hear the last part of her sentences.

'Thank God, thank God she's okay.'

'I'm sorry about Silver, darling. He saved our lives.'

Regaining composure, Mum related how our Border collie, our favourite dog in the world, the dog with a silver streak above one eye, had been alerted to the motorbike which had veered towards them, out of control, while they were on a walk. When he'd sensed the danger, Silver had broken loose from the lead in Mum's hand, knocking her and Christabel out of harm's way. While Mum was bruised, Silver had taken the brunt of the motorbike's force and was killed on impact. The bike's rider had regained control of the bike, and shot off with no concern for his victims.

'Bastard,' I whispered.

Mum had brushed herself down and contacted police. After they arrived, we walked down the road, picked up Silver's body and took him home…

*

I walked from the kitchen on to the veranda.

I looked out at the bright pink flowers in my back garden. They were the only flowers in a garden gorged with the green tints of trees and bushes.

In our special spot, where the pigfaces flowered year after year, lay Silver, our brave dog. It was Silver who made me realise there were beings in our world who made life worth living, who understood, instinctively, the importance of commitment, loyalty, togetherness and dependability…and they were not necessarily human beings.

# Devil's Choice

I was late home – again. I expected trouble. It was her birthday and I'd forgotten in the early-morning rush to get to work.

'Hello, darling,' I said, kissing Jasmine on the cheek.

'Don't darling me,' she replied.

I could tell she wasn't serious. It was her tone. She could pretend very well that she was angry. She was an actress of Academy Award ability.

I often wondered how I'd won her heart. Stunning body, a face to attract a Robert Redford, and hair as lush as any shampoo advert would have you believe. Yet, she'd chosen me. I remember thinking Christmas had come early that April Fool's Day when she'd agreed to my stuttering request for her hand in marriage. She didn't even ask if it was a joke, which I'd expected.

Apologising for my tardiness about recalling her birthday, I presented her with the two dozen roses from behind my back. Her reaction made the struggle with the bouquet through the busy pedestrian traffic all worthwhile. She'd already forgiven me for being late – *and* for forgetting her birthday. She planted a loving kiss on my lips.

'Don't I get one, Daddy?' Matilda, my fifteen-year-old daughter, looked up from her homework.

'Course you do, sweetheart.'

She clasped her arms around my neck and embraced me as if I was the most precious person on earth. No suitor – and there were already plenty of boyfriends I'd had to veto – would ever feel the warmth and tenderness this daughter gave to her father. In looks, she was the clone of her mother, thank God.

But Matilda also had a heart that pumped compassion. She'd already worked out the reason she was on this Earth. Neither Jasmine nor I were happy with our child's chosen purpose. It was her choice to make and she'd decided she would care for orphaned children in Africa. We dreaded the thought of someday being so far apart from our daughter.

I stood back. There they were. Two beautiful human beings. My whole world. Without either, my life would be incomplete. But one of them would have to make a major sacrifice. And it was likely that this would be my choice to make.

*

I first got an inkling something was wrong at the beginning of another year. Fatigue, vomiting, and loss of appetite were regular occurrences. I was aware of these symptoms. I'd been born with one kidney and, from a young age, was told to watch for changes.

The specialist's diagnosis was straightforward. 'The remaining kidney is diseased. When this happens, it cannot be reversed,' he said, sounding as if he were lecturing a hall-full of medical students rather than breaking bad news to an ordinary father facing a life or death situation.

I wanted the good news. There wasn't much.

'Basically, it's end-stage renal disease no longer treatable with conventional drugs. Only two options will allow you to continue living: dialysis or transplant.'

I remembered wanting to hug someone there and then. The specialist had made it clear he would not be the central character in that role play. Instead, I had to wait until I got home where, after breaking the news, Jasmine and Matilda gave me a fair share of cuddling. Their resolve made me resolve to be strong.

*

Dialysis had been more nuisance than painful. But it merely delayed the inevitable.

178

Now, there were no longer options. The transplant had become the only alternative.

'If there are compatible blood group and tissue matches, the success rate is ninety-seven per cent,' the same specialist said, robot like. 'There is a risk for the donor, but it'd be minimal.'

The diagnosis only made the loves of my life stronger.

'I'll see if I'm compatible,' said Jasmine.

She was more than just a beautiful and talented actress, I concluded, not for the first time. I wasn't about to waste time in discussion. I knew the likelihood of her being the right fit was less than minimal.

'So will I,' said Matilda.

'No, you won't,' I replied.

'I'm young and fit – and I'll easily survive with one kidney. You did.'

'No, you won't,' I replied again.

That was my first argument with my beautiful daughter.

Unsurprisingly, they both went to be tested. More surprisingly – the odds against this would've been higher than being born with three kidneys – both were compatible.

Both were also determined. And stubborn. They were clones in so many other respects, besides beauty.

'You're not going to put our daughter's life in jeopardy,' said my wife.

'Mum's bordering on diabetes – you need a younger kidney,' said my daughter.

Neither was budging. I had two donors to keep me living – a wife and a daughter, both of whom I loved in different ways but in equal measures.

It was my choice to make.

Despite the specialist's low-risk assessment for donors of organs, I'd heard some had died in the past.

Insomnia followed, with a question which raged and tormented me night after night: 'Who should I choose?'

The day I decided was the worst of my life.

# A Time Gone By

Miriam Zubabe lived in her mud hut forty years ago when I was a twenty-something. When I drove in the vicinity along a bumpy, country road from one town to another, I used to look down at the valley and see scores of the huts dotting the lush landscape. Sadly, I never stopped to visit. My imagination, however, has allowed me to be transported back forty years.

Finally, I am able to visit the village.

Miriam is there to greet me. She is fluent in English. 'You're not the first person to be surprised by my language skills,' she says. She explains she was always a conscientious student. Every day, she'd walk to and back from school from her family's humble hut. The walk was five kilometres each way.

'In winter, it would be dark when I set off. And the sun would be disappearing behind the hills when I got home,' she says, without remorse. Her resolve paid off, as she achieved marks high enough to attend university.

'I had to live in a rural town near the university,' she says. For three years she lived away from the village to study agriculture, specialising in sustainable farming.

'It must have been difficult to leave your home for that long,' I say.

'It was something I'd factored in when I was young child,' she says. 'I'd decided I would have to forgo family life for a while so I could study further, and then come back and try to implement some of my newfound knowledge in the village. It was only for three years. I was prepared to make a sacrifice for that short amount of time.'

Miriam invites me into the family home. It is like stepping back in time.

We enter through an open space. There is no door. It is a dwarf-sized gap and we bend our backs, like stooped elders, to walk through. The circular hut, with plastered walls and thatched roof, is the size of about eight adult steps, whichever way, from a point in the middle of the room. A large makeshift fireplace is the room's centrepiece.

Miriam explains that the hut is smoke-filled as the fireplace doubles as a stove. It is always operational. Food is cooked on the stove and water warmed so the family can wash themselves before bed. Wood is collected each day by the men to keep the fire burning. Even though it is the middle of the day, inside is as dark as any dusk. Two windows, each about the size of the first black and white TV sets, provide the only light. There are beds to accommodate a family of ten in the space. There is a single bed for Miriam's parents and, for the eight children, there are four bunk beds. They are all village made, and look as if they might collapse.

'I wouldn't like to sleep on the lower bed,' I tell Miriam.

She smiles. 'Luckily, all members of our family are skinny,' she says.

I don't ask about privacy, though I wonder about it. I do ask about the storage space. Or lack of it.

'We don't have many outfits, so no need for storage,' she says. 'Generally, we wear the same clothes every day, and wash them once a week in a stream by the river. It's only a kilometre away. We just wash our undergarments daily.'

'Do you ever wear shoes?' I ask, rudely.

'I don't think Imelda Marcos would be happy to live here,' she responds. 'No room for shoes – there's no need because we go barefoot all of the time.'

'I notice there's no en suite,' I say.

Miriam laughs. 'We've got one loo, which is outside. We share it with three other families, all as large as ours. There's a comparable set-up for almost all of the village occupants.'

'So, Miriam,' I say, 'you go to university in the Big Smoke and you come back, all educated, hoping to practically implement some of your knowledge here?'

'Yes,' she replies, enigmatically.

'Has it happened?'

'No,' she says. 'The village chiefs don't like change. I am a woman too, which is a disadvantage when trying to have a say. I thought I could make a difference, that my knowledge might help to make a difference. It has not happened. Maybe one day that will be the case for someone other than me.' Her fate is accepted with no trace of bitterness.

'So, now what, Miriam? Do you plan to leave?'

'I love it here – it is my home,' she says. 'There's no question I will stay.'

'But you have so much to give the world,' I say.

Instantly, Miriam responds to my lament. 'I give to the world – my world, which is right here. I give in lots of other ways. And I've been lucky enough to receive from my world, too. Shelter. Food. Family. Friends. What more do I really need from the world?'

# First Love

She was the most beautiful girl Jackson Black had ever seen. He could still see her in his mind's eye. She was petite – no taller than half the length of a netball pole – with long, dark hair, curled up at the edges like waves breaking the wrong way around in a restless sea. Her big, brown eyes reminded Jackson of Rolos. He dreamed of devouring them so they'd melt in his mouth. And Mona Lisa would've snarled at this wonder girl's smile. Protecting sparkling white teeth, it would have lit up any arts exhibition.

*

Jackson had just turned eleven – and he was in love. So was every other boy in his primary school. And they were all in love with the same beauty. Or so Jackson believed.

She did not have an exotic name, but Beverley was out of the ordinary. Besotted, Jackson thought about her day and night. He was determined to win her heart, but too shy to explain how he felt. So, he got a friend to tell her.

Later, his friend reported back. Her response was strange. 'She wants you to make her a rabbit cage,' he told Jackson.

Beverley's parents had bought her a bunny and she wanted a special home for her new pet, he explained.

For the first time in his short life, Jackson had to make something with his hands. He was an amateur when it came to building anything, especially a hutch for a rabbit. But, for two weeks, every night, with the help of his patient father, who wasn't any good with his hands either, they put nails to wood, twined wire to ridges, and, finally, put paint to the finished product. It wasn't perfect – it tilted a bit on an even surface – but it was the result, mostly, of Jackson's blood, sweat and tantrums.

Jackson, embarrassed to take his work of art into school, arranged for his busy Dad to drop it off. His father had camouflaged it in a massive kit bag as instructed, because Jackson had wanted it to be a surprise for Beverley.

'It's wonderful, beautiful,' he'd imagined her saying as she unwrapped his gift.

'Just as wonderful and beautiful as you, Beverley,' he'd heard himself reply.

Jackson didn't hand the cage over to Beverley – he'd got his friend to do that – but he had a sleepless night, wondering how she'd rate his handiwork.

At school next day, Jackson was as uptight as a newly captive animal. He still hadn't spoken to the most beautiful girl in the school, but here he was awaiting her verdict on the most elaborate contraption he'd constructed in his life.

Her feedback was revealed through Jackson's friend. She'd asked another boy she'd fancied to build a rabbit's hutch too, and had made her decision.

'She chose the other boy's cage,' said Jackson's friend.

Jackson was told he could pick up his hutch at the school exit where she'd left it, uncamouflaged, in full view of his schoolmates.

Jackson was humiliated. He was devastated for another, more important reason: his beloved Beverley had dumped him, like a discarded mattress, and before he'd even spoken a word to her.

The next morning brought a glimmer of hope for the boy who'd failed. Beverley had reflected on her brutal response. She was prepared to give Jackson another chance to redeem his second-rate construction effort.

Word had got around the school about the contest to win Beverley's heart. It was Angus Dawdle – he of the curly, blond locks – and Jackson who, with this reprieve, were in the running. Literally, it seemed.

The deal was that the two boys would have a race to find the fastest runner. At the finishing line would be Beautiful Beverley. She would be the prize for the boy who was quickest.

On the big day, Jackson turned up, quaking in his Dunlops, behind the school shed. So, too, it appeared, did the rest of the school. It was a contest not to be missed: long-locked Angus versus try-hard Jackson.

It was a fifty-metre race. 'Get ready, get set…' a firecracker went off. So did Jackson. Little legs pumping, gangly arms flaying, he set off… in the windstream left by Angus, who did nothing to live up to his surname.

As Jackson ended his run an eternity after his opponent, he watched Angus and Beverley walk off arm in arm into a sunset brilliant only to the eyes of young lovers. Jackson's reward was a chorus of boos from students who ought to have known better.

Jackson's dream of winning Beverley's heart was over before it had really started. He took days off school to mend his broken heart – and plot his revenge. He contemplated ways he could achieve the latter, like kidnapping Beverley's bunny or breaking into Angus Dawdle's home and cutting off his hair.

*

In the end, Jackson survived this mugging on his youthful sensibilities and was later rewarded by the karma of the universe.

Beverley and Angus eventually married, but divorced after two years.

Jackson married the second most beautiful girl in the school.

After forty contented years, he revels still in his perfect match, despite non-existent handyman skills – and not a rabbit hutch in sight.

# Retreat from Life

'They're all gone, mate, all three of them – we're sorry.'

Simon Joyce looked blankly at the officer who'd broken the news. Stunned, he dropped to the ground. His screams, uncontrolled and savage, broke the silence with the velocity of an airliner at take-off.

*

Simon had always been a shy, reserved boy. He said little at school – and even less at home, where he came from a dysfunctional family, who never showed him a skerrick of love. His mother was addicted to drugs, his father spent more time in the local pub than at home, and his older brother bullied him more than his school mates did.

He'd loathed his brother, even though they'd been left on their own after both parents walked away from their tiny leased unit, leaving the boys to fend for themselves.

In the end, Simon had walked out too, heading to the rented home of a pensioner whom he affectionately called Aunt Betty. She had befriended him on his way to and from school each weekday. A boisterous woman with a wicked laugh, Aunt Betty was the only person who'd showed Simon affection. She made his meals, cleaned after him and kept him company. He appreciated her kindness and the little taste she gave him of what he supposed was a normal life.

Simon, however, preferred to be alone.

That was why it came as a shock to many in Little Rock when Simon met Jane, a plain-looking local girl, fell in love and had a family of his own. No one in the little town where Simon had lived most of his life could quite believe the romance but Simon didn't give a fig for them.

The world, for him, existed within the walls of a small, cheap weatherboard home he'd eventually saved up enough money to buy. That was a world he created for his beloved Jane, just as shy and reserved as he, and their beautiful twin daughters.

Simon had been fortunate to pick up an admin job at the railways. Locals wondered how he'd managed to secure the job. 'He never says a word. He wouldn't have said much in the interview,' said a rival applicant. Some detractors pointed out that Simon's father-in-law happened to be on the interview panel.

Whatever the specifics of landing the job, the money Simon brought in went straight into the coffers of his darling Jane. She was careful with their money, and their daughters' needs always were put before anyone else's.

It was a philosophy Simon wholeheartedly supported. The girls were their lives.

*

The day that became a nightmare had started like any other. Jane hurried the girls over breakfast – and, for once, they'd run out of the house before Simon claimed his usual goodbye kisses and cuddles.

He'd regretted this lapse almost as much as not having them around. Jane, in a rush to get the girls to school on time, had over-corrected on Little Rock's death corner, the one that had claimed so many victims over the years. She'd smashed into a Stobie pole. All three were killed instantly.

While the town came out in hordes for the funeral – there were three white caskets, Jane's in the middle with her twins on either side – Simon was bereft. He immediately resigned his job and, with his only comfort, his collie Kelt (only six months old and bought for his daughters), he packed his Kombi and left town.

For months, Simon scoured the countryside for the spot from which he would retire for good; not only from work, but from life – at the age of forty.

He'd left his house exactly as it was on the day it had lost its soul.

He replaced that with another, much less cared-for home deep in a forest, about a hundred kilometres from a remote town. It was an annexe made of canvas tied up to the Kombi.

'It's just you and me, buddy,' he told Kelt.

That's how it turned out for the rest of Simon's life.

Water was supplied by a river outlet a kilometre from his new home. For the first five years, Simon visited the remote town most fortnights for food. The next five, he went monthly. After that, he lived on crops grown in a makeshift yard and never saw another human being again.

When he died twelve years after the family tragedy – most were sure it was of a broken heart – only Kelt was by his side.

As always, on the night he died, Simon had curled up beside the warped, yellow-stained photograph he had of the only three people in his life he'd loved. He kissed the images of the trio and, cradling the photo to his chest, cuddled it as he'd always done since their deaths.

Simon never saw daylight again.

When he was found by bushwalkers some weeks after his death, they rescued the emaciated Kelt. The dog was traced to Aunt Betty, now in her early seventies, who later received another shock.

In the dozen years since Simon had left his Little Rock property, it had been acquired by an overseas company to start up an open-cut mine. Simon's modest home, sold to him for $80,000, had been bought by the company in his absence for half a million dollars.

That money did not go to his parents or his bullying big brother. Instead, according to the wishes of a will he'd left behind during his search for his hideaway home, it all went to the only person who'd befriended him as a child – Aunt Betty.

Though appreciative of the windfall, life did not change much for the long-time spinster. She spent much of her time nursing Kelt back to full health – in the same way she'd so caringly looked after the faithful dog's master all those years ago.

# The Pencil Case

Rowena Rosewater loved to write. She'd been writing for years, she thought, even though she had just turned eight. Rowena believed she enjoyed writing because her mum was a teacher and more so because her dad wrote long stories for a living.

It was hard for her dad to earn enough to look after their family. However, her mum was happy to go to school each weekday so they could live in a nice house, ride a car that didn't break down and have enough tasty food to feed all three of them.

Rowena wasn't sure when she learned to write. But she knew she could not write without the contents of her pencil case. It was a very special case. It had been in the family for a long time.

It was slender (the width of a tiny arm) and long enough to hold a thirty-centimetre ruler (the length of the side table next to Rowena's bed). The pencil case was made of wood. It had two paper-thin lids, which slid along from one side to the other, though, lately, they sometimes stuck. Faded, flowery patterns coated the lids. Her name was printed in neat capital letters on one of the lids, in permanent ink.

Rowena was protective of her case and would not let anyone touch it – at home or at school.

Inside the case there were five pieces of stationery, always. No more, no less. There were two pencils, both HB of course, a sharpener, an eraser and a ruler, similar in colour to the beige pencil case.

So fond was Rowena of these items that she gave them names.

One pencil was called Polly. It was Polly that Rowena used when she decided to write in cursive. She wasn't as good in cursive as her grandmother or grandfather.

'How'd you keep the bottoms of the letters on the line?' she asked.

'Practice, darling,' said Gran.

'The nuns used to whack me over the knuckles with their wooden rulers so I always made sure my letters sat perfectly on the lines,' said Pops.

So Rowena kept practising to keep her letters neat. When she got annoyed by not keeping the letters on the line, Rowena would cheat – though she didn't think it was cheating – by placing her wooden ruler, which she named Rexie, on the line. She pressed on Rexie firmly with her left hand as she wrote her letters, biting just as firmly on her tongue. She didn't go under the line, but the bottom of the letters would some-times end up looking square instead of round, which also displeased her.

Occasionally, Rowena would draw. When she did that, she used Pixie, the other pencil. This was because Pixie's head, also, of course, made of lead, was darker than Polly's – and Rowena was able to draw black outlines of insects with a firm hand. Often, she'd colour in but-terfly outlines, using crayons from another container.

Sandy, the sharpener, was another piece of stationery Rowena kept in her pencil case. It only contained one blade – she didn't like the bigger, double-bladed sharpeners because they didn't fit properly in her little hand. Rowena was pleased she'd had Sandy the sharpener for all the years she'd been writing, and it had never let her down. She loved the shapes of the fragile shavings as they fell from the blade when she turned the pencils clockwise to ensure a sharp finish. They reminded Rowena of Spanish dancers, twirling their delicate, waving skirts.

Sometimes, if she turned the pencils too quickly, a sliver of lead would fall out of the sharpener, or get stuck in it, and she'd have to start again. She was proud that in her writing career so far that hadn't hap-pened often. She'd had only to replace her favourite pencils two or three times up to now.

Joining her friends in Rowena's pencil case was another favourite: Roley, the rubber. Rowena knew it was actually called an eraser, but she liked the name Roley and therefore called it 'my rubber, Roley'. Rowena would often use Roley, especially if the slanty, top bits of the 'ls' or slanty, bottom bits of the 'ys' weren't as neat as she'd liked. She didn't mind bending her head to blow the bits off her page after she'd vigorously rubbed out letters. She often wondered where those bits had finished up.

*

Rowena Rosewater, the writer, also loved books. That's why the five pieces of stationery in Rowena's pencil case loved school holidays. During four holiday periods each year, Rowena did not use the tools in her precious pencil case. That's because Rowena did not write during the holidays. Instead, she read.

'My friends in the pencil case need time out, too,' she told her mum. 'I use them a lot and they must get as tired as I do. They need to have a holiday, just like me.'

Polly and Pixie, the pencils, ruler Rexie, Sandy the sharpener and rubber Roley were always grateful for – and looked forward to – the school holidays.

They were also rather pleased they had such a kind person as Rowena to care for them. They were quietly confident, too, that she would be a famous writer by the time she was as old as her dad.